Zephyr Spheres and the Silver Unicorn

Myles B. Hibbett

Truman Press

Published by Truman Press

www.trumanpress.us

First Edition: 2024

ISBN: 978-1-963563-00-9

Printed in the United States of America

Contents

Prologue

None could ever remember the beginning of Danus or the birth of magic. Though a part of history, it had long been a knowledge that died generations ago and that was forgotten by all—all but one. A single creature remained that was there since the dawn of creation—a creature that most believed to merely be a myth. The select few who knew of its existence understood that this being was the most magical, beautiful, and mystical alive. But, there was another story of the creature—a secret of which only the three great Oracles of Aeria knew—that the creature was a keeper of an object so powerful that it could change the course of the future. And, only when the beast was tamed, would it reveal its secret to mortal men.

Chapter 1

——◄◦○◦►——

Trinda's Conscious Decision

"**I** can't stand it anymore!" Zephyr said loudly as she threw her sketchbook against the wall in agony. "Every time I try to draw something, it always ends up being the same!"

Walking over to her silver chest, Zephyr peered in the mirror. However, as she observed her dangerously brown eyes, long sparkling silver and midnight black hair, and shimmering cocoa skin, she felt as though she didn't recognize herself.

"Don't be mad, Your Highness," Zephyr's nursemaid, Helga, told her.

The golden-brown skinned dwarf with sapphire eyes, reddish-brown hair tied into two long braids, rosy cheeks with dimples on them, and a red-pointed hat that covered her pointed ears, scurried across Zephyr's bedchambers and picked up her sketchbook.

As Helga gazed at Zephyr's latest sketch, she sighed deeply.

"Still thinking about Prince Cor and Prince Toron I see," she said.

Helga placed the sketchbook beside Zephyr and rubbed her shoulders, and because of the dwarf's small height, she had to step on her toes to do so.

"Yes, Helga," Zephyr said. "I can't help it. Prince Toron is dead, and Cor is in danger. They have both fallen victim to the Dark Forces, and Cor may end up being killed like Toron. It's all my fault."

Zephyr felt very guilty. It was true. She had lived most of her life on Earth with an impoverished foster family known as the Krumples. And, she had only found out a few years ago that she was a sorceress and the Princess of Crystotopia, one of thirteen kingdoms on the world of magic called Danus. Though she had many adventures on the fascinating and wondrous planet, now that she got the chance to stay and not return to Earth for her safety, Crystotopia faced its greatest threat from the evil alliance, the Dark Forces.

In the past, Zephyr had managed to defeat her evil Uncle Otto, the Duke of Eastwood, and Prince Wart of Thunderon, and she also thwarted several plans to take over Crystotopia. But now, at age seventeen, it all seemed like small potatoes to what lay ahead of her.

Several months ago, Zephyr and her friends rescued Queen Astra and Glacionus from the clutches of the Dark Forces and annihilated the tyrant Lodo as well as Queen Mura of Mineralda. They even discovered that Zephyr's guardian, the fire wizard, Cor, was the lost heir and rightful ruler of Ember and the wielder of a power known as the Great Flame.

However, Prince Toron of Sandus was killed trying to protect Zephyr, and just as Zephyr realized that she was in love with Cor, King Scorpius, leader of the Dark Forces, abducted him. Not to mention that the main defense of Crystotopia, the Sword of Wonders, mysteriously disappeared.

Zephyr was in grief over all the bad things that had happened, and she was still recovering from Prince Toron's funeral in Sandus. Now, Prince Sardion, Toron's brother, was to rule in Toron's stead.

"It's alright, Your Highness," Helga said. "You should try to think about the good things and be optimistic. Why just remember that you have helped save Glacionus and now Mineralda as well. Without Queen Mura and Lodo in the way, both kingdoms have been restored to their former glory. And, at least you don't have to go back to that planet, Earth, again. You always wanted to stay in Crystotopia."

"You're right," Zephyr said as she shook her head and closed her eyes. "But I wonder if I should have stayed on Earth with the Krumples. I do detest living with them. But, because of me, so many lives are in jeopardy. And, now that the Sword of Wonders is gone and royal blood has been spilled, a war is about to take place. I just can't help feeling that it's mainly because of me."

Zephyr felt helpless, watching her father, King Lionus II preparing for a battle she didn't think he could win. Though Mineralda had been conquered by the allied kingdoms, rebels still loyal to the deceased Queen Mura and the Dark Forces were posing a threat to Crystotopia and Glacionus. And, with Prince Toron's death, Sandus was also pushing for revenge. Also, now the peace talks were over, and every allied kingdom realized that the Dark Forces and King Scorpius had to be stopped.

The Crystal Castle was bustling with activity. Each day, warriors and volunteers arrived eager to help Crystotopia. Zephyr's father had called forth the aid of all the allied kingdoms as well as the assistance of the Ruby Knights—a group of warriors famed for their combat art. The Ruby Knights were from Warriant, the kingdom of warriors, though they had joined the allied kingdoms to fight against Warriant and its ruler, King Vigor.

So, battle techniques, strategies, practices, and plans were made and carried out. The Crystal Castle was so lively that Zephyr sometimes wondered if she was in a different place.

She came across white centaurs, healers, animal beasts, fairies, dwarves, elves, various wizards and witches of different origins, sorcerers from every part of Danus, small pixies, unicorns, and even pegasi. The diversity seemed endless.

However, although the castle was as hectic as it had ever been, Zephyr and her human friends from Earth: Elizabeth Thompson, Brandon Longfellow, and Trinda Temple, were instructed to stay out of everyone's way. Since going to Earth was no longer an option due to the loss of the Sword of Wonders and the Head Sorcerer of Crystotopia's dimensional key, Zephyr's father and the Chancellor had said that they were trying to decide where on Danus to send Zephyr and her human friends while the war took place.

King Lionus hardly ever slept, and as much as he tried to hide it, his attitude was quite dubious without the Sword of Wonders. In his time, he had never spent a day of his life without feeling somewhat secure because of the sword's presence. But now, he felt quite awkward knowing that the legendary weapon wasn't there to defend his people.

Zephyr and her friends tried very hard to listen to the commands and advice they were given by their elders. However, because of feelings of curiosity, they often found themselves attempting to figure out many of the things that were happening.

It was this curiosity that Zephyr and her friends felt when they decided that they would give up on staying out of the way and take a more prominent role in Crystotopia's situation.

It all began as Zephyr and her friends tried to relax and ignore the events in the Crystal Castle.

Zephyr sat on a bench with Trinda, Brandon, and Liz in the eastern courtyard, in which the castle stable was located. And, Scorn, Zephyr's brown-eyed and brown-feathered falcon to whom she could talk as well as to other animals, was resting on her shoulder.

Trinda possessed caramel skin, soft jet-black curls, and golden eyes. Brandon was thin and muscular with coffee-colored skin. He also possessed deep black eyes and curly dark brown hair. And, Elizabeth was tall with skin the color of oak, forest green glasses, pecan eyes, and dark freckles. She used to wear her black hair in pigtails, but now her hair was wavy and more appealing.

You would think that with everything going on, Zephyr and her friends would be excited. But everything is boring if the affairs taking place are meant to be none of your business. And, Zephyr and her friends were horribly ignored and forgotten.

"We should play a game," Brandon said as everyone stared into space and remained quiet.

"What game can we possibly play without getting in everyone's way?" Liz said. "Every time we even breathe I feel like we are getting on someone's nerves."

"We could try football," Brandon said.

Zephyr, Trinda, and Liz shot him dirty looks.

"Well, it was only a suggestion," Brandon said as he shrugged his shoulders.

"I would give anything to be home right now," Trinda said. "Who knew that we would end up being stuck here? And, what if we get caught up in this war?"

"I wish I could send you home," Zephyr said with a sigh. "If it weren't for me, you guys would be safe back on Earth. I can't leave though. There are too many people I care about here, and part of what is occurring is to due my actions. I have to stay and fight somehow."

"I'd give anything to fight in the war," Brandon said. "Maybe I could fight alongside one of the Ruby Knights."

"War isn't fun Brandon," Liz said. "It never has been fun."

"It doesn't matter anyway," Brandon said. "Everyone here still treats us like we're children."

"You would think that with what we've already done they would look at us differently," Zephyr said. "We've helped battle the Dark Forces before."

"That is not the point," Scorn said as he pecked Zephyr in the head. *"They are trying to keep the people they care about safe and minimize injuries. If any harm should come to you, I know the King wouldn't forgive himself."*

"Yes, Scorn," Zephyr said. *"I know you are right. But this war is our fight too. We aren't children anymore, and they treat us like we don't have a say. We've been in situations that some of the people in this war have never seen. We can do as much as the next person, and we have many reasons to fight ourselves."*

Zephyr lowered her head sadly.

"I have many reasons to anyway," she told Scorn.

Scorn rubbed Zephyr affectionately with his wing as a tear fell down her face. Fortunately, none of her friends seemed to notice that she was crying.

Just then, the stable boy entered the courtyard with several pegasi, and he led them towards the stable.

"Excuse me," Zephyr said.

"Yes, Your Highness," the boy answered.

Unlike Cor, this stable boy had green hair and green eyes, and Zephyr reasoned that he was an earth wizard.

"Has someone arrived?" Zephyr asked.

"Yes," the boy replied as he put his head down. "But, I'm not supposed to tell."

"Oh, but you can tell me," Zephyr said slyly. "I'm the Princess."

"Well," the boy said as he glanced around to make sure no one was watching. "I suppose you're right. As you must know, we were expecting a party to return from Aeria. The King sent messengers to seek the advice of the Oracles as to the whereabouts of the Sword of Wonders. However, the party has yet to come back, and the news is long overdue. But, just now, newly freed dwarves from Mineralda have come."

"Thank you for informing me," Zephyr said.

"You're welcome, Your Highness," the boy said with a bow.

Then, he went back to rounding up the pegasi and leading them into the stable.

"This isn't good," Zephyr said as she faced her friends in despair.

"What do you mean?" Brandon asked.

"The party sent to Aeria hasn't come back," Zephyr told him. "It was probably attacked by the Dark Forces."

"There she goes again," Trinda said as she rolled her eyes. "Always expecting the worst. Why can't you just leave things to your servants? You always want to run off on some adventure and save someone."

Zephyr eyed Trinda irritably, but then she took a deep breath.

"You're right," she said. "That's exactly how Toron got killed. It was because I wanted to help Syphron. Maybe...maybe I'm not fit to be a princess after all."

"Don't be foolish!" Scorn said as he pecked Zephyr and flew to her other shoulder. *"It is a good royal that considers the best and the worst. You're only reasoning."*

"Thanks, Scorn," Zephyr said.

"Zephyr," Liz called. "Don't be so hard on yourself. Trinda was only kidding."

"I was not!" Trinda said defensively, and Liz kicked her hard.

"Ow!" Trinda yelled as she rubbed her leg.

"Look," Liz said. "You may be right about the party being intercepted. It happened before when your father sent expeditions to Thunderon, remember? There is no way to tell if the Dark Forces got to the party or not."

Closing her eyes, Zephyr recalled when her father had sent expeditions to Thunderon to find a cure for a fatal magic-sapping plague that was spreading through Crystotopia.

"Yes, Liz," Zephyr said. "But even if something bad did happen, I can't do anything about it personally. For once, I am going to listen to the advice of my father and the Chancellor."

"I'm glad she sees it my way," Trinda said as she crossed her arms and stood.

Pushing Trinda out of his way, Brandon approached Zephyr.

"Don't say that," he said. "I won't let you. Stop blaming yourself for what happened to Toron and Cor. It couldn't be helped. You did the best you were able to do. And why, just think of all we've done. I never imagined we would save Crsytotopia in the past. But, we did. And, I like it when you follow your instincts. It's a lot more fun."

"But..."

"No buts, Zephyr," Liz said. "I've thought of a good reason for you to go see the Oracles yourself anyway."

"You can't be serious?" Zephyr said.

"I am," Liz said. "I've read quite a bit about the Sword of Wonders in the castle library. Even if the party does return safely, you will still have to go to the location of the Sword of Wonders and retrieve it. The King is busy preparing for war. He can't go after the sword. You're the only one who can go after it. The sword will kill anyone who touches it besides you and your father. "

"Oh!" Zephyr said as she held her throat with surprise. "You do have a point there, Liz. My father can't go after the sword. I am the only one who can bring it safely to Crystotopia."

"Don't tell me you're actually thinking of going off on one of your whimsical journeys?" Trinda said.

"I have to do it," Zephyr said. "And, I'm sure my father will let us go. We'll probably need to have guards with us of course, but I'm positive we can succeed."

"This is insane!" Trinda said loudly as she put her hands on her hips. "There's a war about to set loose, and I want to stay as far away from it as I can when it does. You're on your own!"

"Well...well fine!" Zephyr said in an angry tone. "I don't need you to come with me! I don't even know why I'm telling you anyway! All you care about is yourself, and you're nothing but a spoiled brat!"

As she heard these words, Trinda gave Zephyr a look of utter disbelief.

"You guys are with me aren't you?" Zephyr asked Liz, Brandon, and Scorn.

"To the death!" Brandon said.

"It would seem logical for us to assist you," Liz said. "You're our friend."

"Always," Scorn told Zephyr.

"Thanks," Zephyr said as she shot Trinda a cold glare. "I knew I could count on my friends. My 'real' friends anyhow."

Zephyr walked off to find her father with Scorn on her shoulder, and Brandon and Liz followed close behind her.

If Trinda Temple had been on Earth without her memories of Danus, she most certainly would have ignored Zephyr and gone into hiding at even the mention of battle. But, as she reflected on everything she had been through with Zephyr on her adventures, something inside Trinda made her know that she had to support her no matter how she felt about herself. So, she sighed with frustration as she ran after Zephyr, Brandon, Liz, and Scorn.

"Alright!" she yelled. "I'm coming! I'm going to help you! I don't know why, but I will!"

And with that, Zephyr and her friends prepared for yet another one of their adventures, though it remained to be seen if fate was in their favor.

Chapter 2

Helga's Parents

Zephyr knew her father was most likely in his study. But as she headed towards it, someone stopped her and grabbed her wrist.

Before Zephyr could even see who it was, she lost her balance and fell, and Scorn flew into the air before he rested on her shoulder again.

"Oh, Your Highness! Oh, Your Highness!" a familiar squeaky voice called.

Turning, Zephyr saw her nursemaid sobbing.

"Helga," she said. "Is something wrong?"

"Wrong...wrong?" Helga said. "No, everything is perfect thanks to you.'"

"What's going on?" Liz asked.

She and Brandon helped Zephyr up just as Trinda caught up with them.

"Helga, dear," someone said. "Who is this?"

Looking past Helga, Zephyr spotted two dwarves wearing black pointed hats similar to Helga's red hat. One was a man who had pecan skin, a very large stomach, and sparkling sapphire eyes as well as a long white beard.

The other was a plump and slightly smaller female dwarf with gentle black eyes, golden brown skin, and two reddish brown braids.

"These are my parents!" Helga said happily. "They've just arrived from Mineralda! I haven't seen them in ages, and I didn't know if they were alive or dead!"

Moving towards her parents, Helga pulled Zephyr with her.

"Mother, father, this is who I've been telling you about," she said. "This is Zephyr, Princess of Crystotopia."

"Your Highness," Helga's father said. "At last we meet. It is truly a pleasure." Simultaneously, Helga's father bowed and her mother curtsied.

"We owe you great thanks," Helga's father said. "Many a dwarf has pledged allegiance to Crystotopia after we learned that wicked and greedy woman who thought herself a queen was destroyed. Helga told us of how you helped defeat her. Good riddance!"

"Plowdo, please," Helga's mother said.

"Don't lecture me, Dora," Plowdo said. "She can't do us any harm from the grave!"

"Yes," Dora said. "But she is still our queen. Remember that she was once kind. It was that Dark Magic that rattled her brain. So, bad for you. Very bad indeed. If she would have only let me mix one of my potions, maybe it would have set her wits about her."

"It is an honor to meet you Plowdo and Dora," Zephyr said with a quiet laugh. "Helga has spoken of you and has explained the predicament in which you found yourselves. I am glad to see that you are safe and in good spirits."

"As good as you can be in after serving Mura," Plowdo said. "Blast her soul! She had us dwarves mining night and day, sometimes with little or no food or water. And for what?! Just to fill her newest treasury and fatten her pockets!"

Dora approached Zephyr and whispered softly.

"Don't mind him, Your Highness," she said. "He's very sore about what Queen Mura did, enslaving us and all. But, he's not that upset, and he's really quite happy to be free. That I can tell you."

"You see," Helga told Zephyr. "This is part of the optimism. Some of the good that has come of your great deeds."

"I helped too you know!" Trinda said quickly, and Liz shot her a look that made her take a step back and quiet down.

"Have you introduced your parents to Limpo and Zimpo?" Zephyr asked. "And of course, you must introduce them to Gusto."

"Oh my!" Helga said. "Where has my head gone? How could I forget my friends and Gusto? Oh, mother, he's just dreamy. We've been dating for quite a while now. He's the Master Chef of the castle kitchen you know."

"He sounds lovely," Dora told her.

"I don't like the sound of him one bit!" Plowdo said. "Gusto sounds so iffy! And, you didn't tell me you were dating this fellow! He seems quite suspicious to me! How long have you known him?!"

"Come along," Helga said. "I'm sure you will like him once you meet him, and there's still brother Limpo and brother Zimpo as well."

"Are you dating them too?!" Plowdo asked.

Helga and her mother giggled softly as they walked off with Plowdo.

"There you are," Scorn told Zephyr. *"There is some good that has come of your actions. But, you can't expect everything to go your way. Nothing is perfect, and nothing lasts forever."*

"True indeed, Scorn," Zephyr replied. *"Come, let's find my father."*

Walking off, Zephyr motioned to her friends.

"Come on you guys," she called to Brandon, Trinda, and Liz, and they went after her.

However, when Zephyr reached the entrance to her father's study, she came across a large crowd and mass of people, and messengers, generals, and royal court members filled the corridor outside. Zephyr reasoned that if she waited her turn to see her father it would likely take days before she finally got to speak to him.

"What are we going to do?" she asked her friends quietly. "We'll never get to talk to my father at this rate."

"Well I'm not going to wait that long," Brandon said quickly.

Moving forward, he started to shove his way through the crowd. But a second later, a huge man with bulging muscles who was dressed in red armor and a red cape, picked Brandon up by his shirt as he tossed him backwards, and Brandon landed at Zephyr's feet.

Observing the man, Zephyr saw that he was bald with skin the color of coal. Also, he had topaz eyes, and there was a scar over his left cheek.

"Hey!" Brandon called.

"Wait your turn boy!" the man said. "The Ruby Knights have waited hours to speak to the King just like everyone else! Be patient!"

Zephyr, Liz, and Trinda broke into laughter.

"It's not funny!" Brandon said. "I almost made it! Besides, I'm just as important as he is!"

"Okay," Liz said. "Let me try to solve this problem. I'm sure logic is the key. Now, let me think."

Elizabeth put her finger on her chin as she entered deep thought. Then, she jumped as an idea crossed her mind.

"I've got it!" she said. "We need a distraction! Something to make everyone turn his attention away from the King's study."

"Maybe if Scorn flies over their heads," Zephyr said.

"No," Liz said. "Someone might think Scorn is a threat and attack him."

"Then, what on earth do you expect us do?" Trinda asked loudly.

Zephyr, Liz, and Brandon looked at her and then smiled at each other.

"Oh great!" Trinda said with a sigh. "Leave it to the fabulous, noble, and humble Trinda Temple to get her friends out of a jam!"

Zephyr, Liz, and Brandon backed away from Trinda as they inched towards the King's study.

Then, suddenly, Trinda threw herself to the ground and screamed, and everyone in front of the study turned and ran to her side.

The Ruby Knight who had scolded Brandon reached Trinda first as he helped her up.

Pushing her hand through her soft jet-black curls, Trinda winked at Zephyr, Brandon, and Liz.

"Fair maiden," the Ruby Knight said to Trinda. "Are you injured?"

"Oh!" Trinda said as she covered her forehead with her hand. "I've had a horrible fright, and I've fallen and hurt myself."

"Don't worry, My Lady," the Ruby Knight said. "I, Sir Gallan, shall see that you are well taken care of."

"Perhaps you should take the girl to the castle's healers' quarters," someone suggested.

"Oh thank you kind gentlemen," Trinda said.

While everyone was occupied with Trinda, Zephyr, Liz, and Brandon tiptoed into the King's study.

Zephyr found once she was inside that parchment and books littered the floor, and she had never seen her father's study in such mayhem.

The Chancellor was having a heated discussion with the King, and it was so heated, that neither the Chancellor nor Zephyr's father noticed that Zephyr and her friends had entered the room.

Zephyr's father possessed light black hair, cocoa skin, as well as warm brown eyes.

The Chancellor had neatly trimmed hair the color of freshly paved blacktop, cold black eyes, a perfect goatee, and orange-brown skin.

"The party will arrive!" the Chancellor said. "Do not worry Lionus, I've sent the best messengers and guards to carry out this mission. I am sure that the Dark Forces probably don't even know that we are seeking advice from the Oracles."

"I don't want to hear it, Robart," the King said. "Even if the party does return, it won't hurt to send another one to Aeria. We have to take precautions."

"But Sire," the Chancellor said. "We need everyone here. We are preparing for battle, and Crystotopia can't afford to send out another party."

Suddenly, Brandon accidentally knocked over a glass statue of a unicorn, and its horn broke off as it fell to the floor.

Turning to the source of the commotion, the King and the Chancellor faced Zephyr and her friends, and the Chancellor shot Zephyr a cold glare.

"What are you doing here?!" he said angrily. "How dare you! I thought I told you and your little friends to stay out of the way!"

Gliding across the room, the Chancellor picked up the broken unicorn statue.

"You can see why I told you to do so," he said as he held up the statue.

"It's alright," the King said. "I'm sure my daughter has a good reason for coming to see me."

"I...I do father," Zephyr said as she approached the King nervously.

She hadn't seen her father in weeks, not even at meal times. And, as she gazed upon him, Zephyr could only muster thoughts of concern.

The King's eyes were bloodshot, and he seemed worn and tired. Also, his hair was a ragged mess.

"Yes, Zephyr, whatever is the matter?" he asked.

"I'm sorry to trouble you but um..."

"We wish to send a party including ourselves to retrieve the Sword of Wonders, Your Majesty," Liz said as she interrupted Zephyr.

"What?!" the Chancellor said.

He was so shocked that he nearly fell backward.

"This can't be! Can't you just behave for once and act like a normal princess?!"

"Why, why do you wish to do such a thing?" the King asked.

"It was Elizabeth's idea really," Zephyr said. "She figured that you were busy with preparations for the war, and...and...."

"Go on," the King said.

"Well, she thought that because I'm your only living blood relative, that I have to retrieve the sword. I'm the only one who can touch it besides you. And, I would want my friends to go with me to complete the task."

"Preposterous!" the Chancellor said loudly. "We can't let you go searching for the King's sword! It is much too dangerous! The nerve..."

"That's enough!" the King said as he cut off the Chancellor.

Then, he peered into Zephyr's eyes.

"The Chancellor does have a point, daughter," he said. "It would be extremely dangerous for you to attempt such a journey."

"We can handle anything the Dark Forces will dish out!" Brandon said.

"Humph!" the Chancellor mumbled as he folded his arms.

"Brandon's right, in a way, father," Zephyr said. "My friends and I have faced the Dark Forces before. And, haven't we proven that we are reliable?"

"Well," the King said as he sat back in his chair. "You also make a good point. But, that doesn't mean you will be successful on this quest. The Dark Forces are stronger than ever. You may have been lucky in the past, but this time might be different. I'm sorry, but I can't let you do it. I'm sure we can manage without putting you and your friends in the line of fire."

"Your Majesty," Liz said as she moved towards the King's desk. "Although it is dangerous, you must reconsider. The party you sent to Aeria has yet to come back, and the Dark Forces have taken actions to intercept your messengers before. Plus, there is no way that you can leave the kingdom to search for the Sword of Wonders. Zephyr is your best chance of getting the sword back. Even if the location of the sword is discovered, you and Zephyr are the only people who can touch it. It makes perfect sense to send her to retrieve it. Why, it's the most logical solution."

"Hmm," the King said under his breath.

Rubbing his chin, he stared blankly into space.

"You're right," he said with a sigh after a minute.

"Your Majesty!" the Chancellor bellowed. "This is ridiculous! Surely, they will be killed!"

"Perhaps you would like to go in my stead or accompany me, Chancellor?" Zephyr asked as her eyes sparkled.

As he stared at Zephyr, the Chancellor reddened with rage.

Then, he stormed out of the room, and Zephyr chuckled just as she cleared her throat and glanced at her father.

"I will assemble an escort to join you and your friends on your quest," the King said. "However, before you search for the location of the Sword of Wonders, it is imperative that you seek the advice of the Oracles. I fear the worst has befallen the party I sent to Aeria a few weeks ago. Therefore, you must go there first."

Scorn flapped his wings happily as he pecked Zephyr gently.

"Yes, father," Zephyr said. "I will not fail you."

Together, Zephyr and her friends grinned as they left the King's study. And, as soon as they were gone, the King put his head down and took a deep breath.

"Oh, Andromeda," he said to himself. "My worst fears are confirmed. No matter how much I try to keep her safe, she must fulfill her destiny."

Chapter 3

The Journey Begins

Zephyr spent the next few days preparing for her journey. She waited patiently to find out who would be joining her and her friends on their quest, though Zephyr's father evaded her questions about the subject. It wasn't until the day she was to leave that she found out exactly with whom she would be traveling.

Zephyr, Trinda, Brandon, and Elizabeth stood in the main courtyard, and Scorn sat on Zephyr's arm. Zephyr, Trinda, and Liz were dressed in white body suits, and Brandon was dressed in a blue mail. Also, everyone wore black cloaks.

Zephyr was armed with her weapon of the art of Chimmera, named Wind Chaser, and she wore the silver-heart-shaped locket containing a picture of her mother that was a gift from her father as well as the thin golden friendship bracelet that she received from Cor—both for luck.

Liz was armed with a yellow glowing crystal spear, Trinda had a gray glowing crystal bow and quiver of arrows, while Brandon carried a blue glowing crystal sword.

Together, they sat still on benches until Zephyr's father was to arrive with their escort.

But much to Zephyr's surprise, meeting her escort was more like a reunion of old allies with whom she had gone on previous adventures.

Several black horses with bags of horse-feed and flasks of water attached to their saddles were brought into the courtyard along with one that Zephyr immediately recognized as being a mare named Tarn. Tarn was the horse that Zephyr rode on her journey to Letros' lair in Thunderon.

"Tarn!" Zephyr said happily, and she gently patted the horse on the back. *"It's so good to see you."*

"I'm glad to see you, too," Tarn replied. *"It gets so lonely with no one to talk to."*

After the horses, Syphron, the Head Sorcerer of Crystotopia arrived. He was a man with pine-colored skin, striking gray eyes, a hairless head, and he always wore ten magic variously jeweled golden rings on his fingers.

Then, much to Zephyr's delight, Helga and her parents, her boyfriend, Gusto, as well as Limpo and Zimpo also showed up.

Gusto was a dwarf with mahogany skin, emerald green eyes, and a light brown beard.

And, Limpo and Zimpo were twin dwarven brothers with pecan skin. However, Limpo possessed brown eyes, while Zimpo's eyes were purple.

Next, Little Herb and his parents came into the courtyard. Little Herb was a healer who just like other healers had blue skin, frizzy green hair, and black eyes, and he had also helped Zephyr travel to Thunderon and to Letros' lair.

Following Little Herb and his parents, the white centaurs, Valon, Cara, Piro, and Trion appeared. All white centaurs had blue hair, blue glowing eyes, and white skin. However, Piro was heavyset, Valon was thin and lanky, Trion was short, and Cara was a female centaur dressed in white armor. The white centaurs had worked with Zephyr and her friends to save Glacionus from Lodo and Queen Mura and restore Queen Astra to her throne. Now, armed with wooden spears possessing metal tips, the white centaurs stood before Zephyr once more ready to come to her aid.

Then finally, Zephyr's father and the Chancellor entered the courtyard along with a Ruby Knight, who Trinda recognized as being Sir Gallan. They were followed by several fairy guards, each with white eyes and pairs of wings.

The fairy guards wore silver armor that covered their heads and chests, but below their waists, they wore white and gold kilts. On their feet, there were matching white slippers lined with silver. The only main difference between the fairy guards' appearances was the color of the crystal spears they carried.

However, Zephyr somehow immediately recognized two of the fairy guards. There was Peantos holding a green glowing crystal spear, who was the first fairy guard Zephyr had ever met, and there was also Thantos holding a blue glowing crystal spear, who Zephyr knew was Peantos' friend.

But Zephyr didn't know the third fairy guard, who held a white glowing crystal spear.

"Father," Zephyr said. "What is all this? Are all these people going with us?"

"No, daughter," the King replied. "Some of these people just insisted that they say good-bye to you and your party. However, I tried to form an escort that you were somewhat familiar with. Also, the Ruby Knight, Sir Gallan, has requested that he travel with you."

The King pointed to Sir Gallan, who was dressed in his red armor and cape, and he quickly winked at Trinda, who immediately blushed.

"We've met," Brandon said in a dry tone.

He recalled being tossed onto the ground by the knight.

"There are also the white centaurs," Zephyr's father said. "Valon, Cara, Trion, and Piro."

"We are here to serve you, Your Highness," Trion said as the centaurs bowed. "We are still in your debt for you returning Queen Astra to her throne."

"There is the healer, Little Herb," Zephyr's father said.

Little Herb bowed with a smile, and Zephyr laughed.

"An amateur healer at your service no longer," Little Herb said. "Well...at least an intermediately skilled one now anyway."

"And the fairy guards," the King said.

"Peantos, Thantos, and Reen," he said as he pointed to the fairy guards. "They have volunteered to go with you."

"It is an honor," Reen said as he bowed and raised his white glowing crystal spear.

"Your nursemaid, Helga, insisted that she help you as well," the King said.

"But, Helga," Zephyr said as she faced the dwarf. "You should stay with your family and friends. You've only just found your parents."

"My duty foremost is to serve you, Your Highness," Helga said. "Now, that I have my family back, I realize that it is partially thanks to you. So, I want to help. Whatever you need."

Helga hugged Zephyr tightly, and Zephyr peered at her father with joy.

"I have given some thought to what you and your friends told me," he said with a smile. "And, you are absolutely correct. You have faced the Dark Forces, and you have succeeded where so many have failed. That is why I have gathered many of your old allies. I figured that you should be surrounded by those who helped you in the past. They were successful then, and they might be again."

"Thank you, father," Zephyr said as she hugged the King.

"Yes," the Chancellor said as he rolled his eyes. "The King thought it would be a good idea to select those who previously aided you for your escort."

"Isn't it grand?" he said sarcastically.

"You must go quickly and return just as swiftly," the King said.

"I am giving you a thousand gold and a thousand silver lucans should you need any money," Zephyr's father told her as he handed her several heavy sacks of coins.

"I have prepared the best food possible for such a journey," Gusto told Zephyr. "Only the best for my Helga. I would go too, but the King thinks he needs my help to feed the armies and keep them satisfied."

Together, Helga, Gusto, and the fairy guards attached several satchels of food to the saddles of the horses and onto the white centaurs' backs.

"Oh, hogwash!" Plowdo said as he turned his head. " Mr. Master Chef, Gusto, is probably scared!"

Laughing, Helga patted her father on the back.

"I will miss you," she said.

"Be careful, daughter," Dora said as she hugged Helga.

Little Herb's parents also hugged and kissed him goodbye.

Then, Syphron put his hand on Zephyr's shoulder.

"Oh, Syphron," Zephyr said as she held his hands and looked at him.

Standing back, she sighed deeply.

"What is it?" Syphron asked.

"It's just," Zephyr said. "Now that all my friends are here, I have no idea what the outcome of this quest will be. I don't know how everything is going to turn out, and you never do with a war involved. How will I know that Crystotopia and the people I care about that I'm leaving behind will be safe?"

"I see," Syphron said as he rubbed his chin, and after a second, he snapped his fingers.

"I know a way that you can!" he said. "Have you heard of an enchantment that lets you see what your bonding creature sees?"

"Well, uh, yes," Zephyr said. "I used it to escape from Prince Wart's castle. Scorn is my bonding creature."

"Just as I thought," Syphron said. "Wait here!"

Turning, he hurried into the castle. And soon, he came back twenty minutes later carrying a small silver ring with a white crystal in the center of it as well as a silver necklace that had a small white crystal attached to it.

"That ring looks just like the one Scorn gave me," Zephyr said.

She recalled the magic ring she had used to grant her wish to attend her junior prom back on Earth. She ended up taking Cor with her and winning a dance competition that made her Prom Queen.

"This possesses another type of magic crystal," Syphron said as he handed Zephyr the ring.

"Put it on," he said.

Zephyr did as Syphron instructed, and he placed the silver necklace around Scorn's neck. Then, Syphron twisted all the rings on his fingers, and he grabbed the necklace Scorn was wearing and the ring Zephyr had put on as he began to chant softly. But, Zephyr couldn't even make out what he was saying.

Slowly, the crystals of the ring and the necklace began to glow a bright gray in unison with each other.

"Now," Syphron told Zephyr. "Cast the enchantment."

"Alright," Zephyr said as she took a deep breath.

Closing her eyes, she ran, "Sightus Impetus Executo!" through her mind, and she waved her hand.

Suddenly, with her eyes closed, Zephyr could see Syphron and everyone standing in front of her. Only, she could tell that she was seeing through Scorn's vision.

Opening her eyes, Zephyr broke the spell.

"What...what is this?" she asked.

"Wherever you are," Syphron said. "Just say the magic words to the Sight for Sight enchantment, and you will be able to see through Scorn's eyes. And, whenever you open your own eyes, the spell will break. But if you wish, you may perform the spell again when you please."

"But, how is this working?" Zephyr asked. "How can the spell work anywhere? Isn't there a limit to how far away from each other we can be?"

"No, Princess," Syphron said. "You must remember that magic crystals can enhance spells. Through the magic and connection of the crystals I have given you and Scorn, the spell will work no matter how far apart you two are as long as you both stay on Danus and there is little magical interference. Let Scorn stay with me, and you can see through him and communicate to him with your thoughts to find out how everyone is doing at any time."

"Oh, Syphron!" Zephyr said. "You're a genius!"

"Is it okay if you stay with Syphron, Scorn?" Zephyr asked her falcon.

"Of course," Scorn replied. *"I can't wait to sink my talons into members of the Dark Forces. A battle cannot scare me away."*

Zephyr kissed Scorn gently on his head, and he flapped his wings as he flew to Syphron's shoulder.

"We must make haste and stop saying goodbyes," Little Herb said. "We have a long journey ahead of us. We have to go through Vainaquia before we reach the Great Stair and Aeria. I have maps showing a path on land that we can take through the water kingdom, but we must be careful. Vainaquia has spies. It is a kingdom allied with the Dark Forces after all."

"Yes," Zephyr said as she mounted Tarn's back. "We have to get going."

Liz got onto Tarn's back as well as she held Zephyr's waist.

"I still haven't gotten used to horseback riding," she said.

"Neither have I," Brandon said as he mounted a horse with Trinda.

"Children!" Sir Gallan said with a snort as he mounted a horse. "I'm escorting helpless children!"

Trinda eyed Sir Gallan carefully, and he cleared his throat.

"Uh, not you, of course, My Lady," he said. "I mean the boy."

"Yeah right!" Brandon said as he rolled his eyes.

Helga and Little Herb rode on Trion's back. And, the fairy guards flew beside the horses and the white centaurs.

Then, before another word was said, Zephyr and her new party waved to their friends and family and rode off away from the Crystal Castle, not knowing what risks and perils they might encounter. They tried to focus on their goal—to find the location of the mysterious Sword of Wonders and bring it back to Crystotopia before the allied kingdoms' armies could be defeated by the Dark Forces.

Chapter 4

A Discovery in Eastwood

Zephyr and her party traveled hastily through Crystotopia. Aeria was in the west past Vainaquia, and Zephyr's party had to go through the forests of Eastwood to reach Vainaquia's border.

As everyone moved through the darkened tree-lined section of Crystotopia, Zephyr cringed as memories raced through her mind of her wicked Uncle Otto, the Duke of Eastwood.

The last time Zephyr was in Eastwood, she had to confront her uncle at his castle to save her father and Crystotopia.

"This forest gives me chills," Zephyr said as she rubbed her shoulders.

"It's so...so dark," Trinda said. "It could definitely use a trimming at the very least. The light is hidden by these towering trees."

"Stay close and do not wander," Sir Gallan said.

"Why are you worried about this place, Your Highness?" Helga asked Zephyr. "The Dark Forces were driven from here after you defeated your uncle."

"I know," Zephyr said. "But that doesn't make it safe. I have a funny feeling about Eastwood."

"This forest bothers me too," Tarn said. *"Remember, I'm a bit claustrophobic, and this place has cramped written all over it."*

"I have the same feeling, Tarn," Zephyr replied. *"And I'm not normally afraid of tight spaces."*

Just then, Sir Gallan stopped, and he held up his hand as he motioned to Zephyr and her friends.

"Hey!" Brandon said. "What's the holdup?!"

"Quiet!" Sir Gallan said. "There's something watching us! Just ahead behind that group of trees."

Everyone stopped and stayed still, and Zephyr held her breath as she saw the tree branches in front of Sir Gallan beginning to shake.

Moving forward slowly, Sir Gallan unsheathed a long broad sword.

Then, Trion, Piro, Cara, and Valon surrounded the moving tree branches as they readied their spears for attack.

However, a cawing crow emerged from the trees and flew off into the distance.

"A crow!" Trinda said loudly. "You had me scared for nothing! There isn't anything out there!"

But suddenly, everyone heard the nearby sound of a twig snapping.

"Hurry," Sir Gallan whispered. "Behind those bushes."

The Ruby Knight pointed to a group of tall and rich green bushes to the right, and Zephyr and her party scurried behind them as they tried to stay hidden and still.

And then, two giant trolls with clubs came into sight—heavyset creatures with light green skin and warts all over their bodies, as well as yellow eyes, and ragged black hair. Also, Zephyr immediately noticed their familiar stench of dead animals.

"Me told you there was nothing over here!" one of the trolls said. "Just a birdie!"

"Me know I heard voices," the other troll said. "Somewhere be people that we cook for dinner."

"Stupid!" the first troll said as he hit the second lightly on the head with his club. "Your stomach talks too much! Nothing here! We now go report to Prince Wart, King Vigor, and King Seadon's general."

Turning, the trolls disappeared into the forest.

"Trolls," Helga said with a gasp. "What are they doing here?"

"I don't know Helga," Zephyr said as she narrowed her eyes. "But, I'm going to find out."

Dismounting Tarn and standing, Zephyr ran off in the direction the trolls had gone.

"Zephyr, stop," Liz whispered. "We need to avoid the trolls, not go where there are probably more of them."

But Zephyr ignored Liz as she struggled to force her way past tree branches and bushes and go deeper into the forest.

"Oh no!" Zephyr suddenly said with a quiet gasp.

What she stumbled onto shocked her terribly and made her wish that she had listened to Elizabeth. Backing up, she threw herself behind a tree to hide.

Then slowly, she peered around the tree to observe the horrible sight she had discovered.

Trolls and various other beasts surrounded her Uncle Otto's old castle—a structure made of dark black rock.

There were goblins—green and brown creatures with snouts, fangs, and fierce white eyes.

There were water wizards with blue hair, gills, and webbed feet, as well as what Zephyr guessed were walking fish.

There were also trackers—creatures with yellow glowing eyes, sabers, and lizard-like bodies.

And, for the first time, Zephyr saw ogres, and she only knew them from her studies of magic. They were giant man-eating creatures with daggers for teeth, dirty black skin, red eyes, and tufts of red hair on their heads.

Also, there were various other warriors and soldiers dressed in armor.

Zephyr tried to get a sense of how many evil minions were lurking about, but it seemed like at least three armies. Tents were stationed inside and out of the castle, and Zephyr could see the remains of several dead fairy guards.

Turning quickly, she started to head back to her party.

But before Zephyr could make her way into the forest, something snarled grabbed the back of her cloak and threw her to the ground.

Peering up, Zephyr spotted a muscular warrior in thick green armor, and she noticed that he had dirty tan skin, menacing black eyes, and long dark black hair.

"Well, well!" he said. "What have we here?! A little spy, perhaps?! You've seen a bit too much! But don't worry, you won't see anything again!"

Raising his sword high in the air, the warrior was about to strike.

But running "Freezus Executo!" through her mind as fast as she could, Zephyr whirled her hands, and a blue beam of light hit the warrior in the stomach and pushed him back a few inches.

"Oh, a sorceress we have here!" the warrior said with a laugh. "You should be smart enough to know that Warrianthian knights wear magical armor."

The warrior brought his sword down, and Zephyr shrieked and turned her head at her impending doom.

"TWANG!"

Zephyr heard the heavy clanging of metal, and she looked up to see Sir Gallan warding off the evil warrior's attack with his long broad sword.

"Not so fast!" Sir Gallan said.

Raising his sword, he forced the evil warrior backward.

"The Ruby Knight, Sir Gallan!" the evil warrior said with a hiss. "So, you've betrayed King Vigor to protect little girls!"

"Anything is better than serving that lout!" Sir Gallan said. "King Vigor lost his mind years ago, and he won't stop until every bit of Danus is in flames! You are a fool to follow him, Sir Waian!"

Grunting, the evil knight started swinging his sword at Sir Gallan. However, the Ruby Knight ducked and charged at Sir Waian, and their swords ended up clashing.

"You traitors are no match for the Emerald Knights!" Sir Waian said.

Raising his hand, he did a palm thrust that struck Sir Gallan in the chin and knocked him off of his feet.

"Guards!" Sir Waian yelled. "Trespassers!"

Zephyr ran, "Earthus Maximus Executo!" through her mind and waved her fingers. The ground started shaking so violently that it cracked and a rift appeared, and Sir Waian and the other evil minions close to him were forced to lose their balance. Without a moment to lose, Zephyr helped Sir Gallan up.

"We've got to get away from here!" she said loudly.

Together, she and the Ruby Knight took off into the forest. Zephyr was so busy looking over her shoulder to see if she was being followed that she ran right into Brandon, and they both fell backward.

"Watch it!" Brandon said as he rubbed his swollen forehead.

"We have to get moving!" Zephyr said frantically. "There are armies camping out at my uncle's castle, and they're onto us!"

Just as she spoke, an arrow struck a tree above Zephyr's head.

"Why didn't you say so sooner?!" Trinda said anxiously.

Mounting their horses and the white centaurs, Zephyr and her friends took off, and Peantos, Thantos, and Reen provided cover as they soared through the air.

"Hurry Tarn!" Zephyr told her horse as she held onto her mane. *"This is a life and death situation!"*

"I'm going as fast as I can under these conditions!" Tarn said with a pant. *"Horses do much better in open fields and pastures! In this dreary place, you have to look before you step!"*

"Oh I wish I had stayed home, Your Highness," Helga said with a whimper. "I didn't know we would end up running for our lives!"

"But Sir Gallan is with us," Trinda said. "We shouldn't have anything to fear."

"You won't even be able to feel fear any longer if the Emerald Knights catch us!" Sir Gallan said.

Just then, a group of trackers jumped out and cut off the party's path.

Fortunately, Zephyr acted quickly as she flashed, "Freezus Maximus Executo!" through her head and waved her hand.

And, as Sir Gallan came upon the trackers with his horse, they froze, and the Ruby Knight swiped his sword sideways as he shattered the frozen trackers to pieces.

Without looking back, Zephyr and her friends hurried through the rest of Eastwood, and they didn't stop moving until they got to the forest's edge, which was a sign that they had reached Crystotopia's border.

Ahead of them, instead of the trees and bushes of Eastwood, lay the beaches of Vainaquia and the endless watery depths and giant sea of the kingdom.

Darkness had fallen upon the sky, and multicolored stars as well as the three moons of Danus shone brightly.

"We should rest here," Sir Gallan said. "We have run long enough. I don't think the Dark Forces will stray far from their camp."

Dismounting their horses and the white centaurs, Zephyr and her friends relaxed on the sand, and Zephyr suddenly felt calm as the serene sound of the rushing waves on the beach surrounded her.

"How did those armies get into Crystotopia?" she asked. "We have to warn my father."

"Without the King's sword," Sir Gallan said. "The Dark Forces can attack the kingdom in large numbers with no one knowing."

"I fear that even a healer won't be able to help the allied kingdoms if King Lionus is not told of this threat," Little Herb said.

He started to give the horses some horse feed and water, while Helga unpacked sandwiches that Gusto had made for the rest of the party.

"Those trolls said something about King Vigor, Prince Wart, and King Seadon's general," Zephyr said. "I think they are stationed at my uncle's castle with their armies."

"Not to mention the Emerald Knights," Sir Gallan said. "They mean trouble, and I suspect that the Dark Forces have soldiers positioned at each section of Crystotopia's borders. North, west, east, and south. They will have better chances of capturing the kingdom if they attack from all sides."

33

"And everyone at the Crystal Castle is a sitting duck," Helga said. "My parents, Gusto, brother Zimpo, and brother Limpo. They will all be captured...or even killed."

"What about those Emerald Knights?" Trinda asked Sir Gallan. "Why are you afraid of them? They are knights just like you."

"Even the white centaurs of Glacionus know of the Emerald Knights," Trion said.

"Long ago," Sir Gallan said softly. "The Ruby Knights were the strongest and most loyal warriors on Danus. They were the right arm of King Vigor. Each Ruby Knight was taken from his family as a youth and taught the secret battle techniques and virtues of the King. This was, of course, before King Vigor went mad, and many battles were won thanks to the Ruby Knights. But one day, King Vigor became tempted by the Dark Forces. Warriant was threatened, for King Scorpius sought to control the kingdom's warriors and learn their battle skills. At first, Warriant fought Scorpius, but the Dark Forces only seemed to grow in power. So, out of panic and admiration, King Vigor joined the Dark Forces and began to delve into Dark Magic. It was a grave mistake, for King Vigor went mad and declared war against the allied kingdoms. Then, he started to send the Ruby Knights to fight battle after battle consistently. It soon became clear that all the ethics and morals that the Ruby Knights were taught by King Vigor were no longer important to him. War is not about destroying the world. It is about proving your worth and fighting for what noble cause in which you believe. King Vigor only wanted to see bloodshed for his enjoyment. So, the Ruby Knights had to leave his side, or Vigor would have led us to not only our destruction but through us, the destruction of countless others."

Sighing, Sir Gallan lowered his head sadly.

"But, what does that have to do with the Emerald Knights?" Brandon asked.

"Ah lad, that is the worst part of the story," Sir Gallan said. "With the Ruby Knights gone, King Vigor began to train new youths to be knights of a different breed. He no longer taught ethics, morals, and right from wrong. He taught these recruits the most ruthless and destructive battle strategies and skills he could, and he gave them a one-track mind. Chivalry no longer mattered. All the Emerald Knights think of is their own well-being, killing, and destroying. That is their one purpose of living until they give their last breath in battle. Out of everyone on Danus, the Ruby Knights fear no one except for the Emerald Knights and King Vigor himself. No matter which you meet first, it will be a battle to the death."

"That sounds awful," Zephyr said. "But, we have to go back. We have to warn my father, somehow."

Standing, Zephyr faced the forest, but Liz blocked her path.

"Wait!" she said loudly. "There is another way, Zephyr!"

"What?" Zephyr said as she wrinkled her brow.

"Don't you remember the crystal ring Syphron gave you? You can warn your father through Scorn."

"Of course!" Zephyr said with wide eyes. "Scorn can hear my thoughts through the bonding animal enchantment. Thanks, Liz."

Raising her finger, Zephyr touched her crystal ring and closed her eyes.

"Sightus Impetus Executo!" she thought, and she whirled her hand.

Then suddenly, Zephyr could see the familiar walls of the Crystal Castle, and there were several men and women dressed in flamboyant clothing and capes, who Zephyr guessed were members of the Council of Sorcerers.

"Scorn!" Zephyr thought. "Can you hear me?!"

"Yes," Scorn replied. "Is all well?"

"No," Zephyr thought. "We discovered that Eastwood has Prince Wart's, King Vigor's, and King Seadon's armies in it. We've managed to escape, but you have to tell Syphron about it and have him warn my father. Sir Gallan thinks that the Dark Forces will attack from the north, west, east, and south areas of Crsytotopia's borders. Tell them, Scorn. Please, I'm counting on you."

"I will do as you wish, Zephyr. Take care!"

Opening her eyes, Zephyr broke the enchantment, and she peered at her friends.

"Did it work, Your Highness?" Helga asked eagerly.

"Yes, Helga," Zephyr said. "I think so."

"Then, you and your friends should relax now, " Cara said. "We white centaurs are used to getting little sleep, so we will take turns and keep watch throughout the night."

"We will keep guard as well," Peantos said as he nodded to Thantos and Reen. "We are royal guards, and we do not know how skilled you white centaurs are at keeping watch."

"Better than you I'm sure," Trion said with a grunt. "You forget that we are royal guards as well, and I am sure our training is superior to yours.'"

"We can test that notion and see who the best guards are right now!" Thantos said angrily.

Moving forward, he was prepared to fly and charge at Trion.

"Enough!" Zephyr said as she pushed Thantos and Trion apart. "We have to work together! No fighting! You can both help keep watch! Four eyes are better than two anyway."

"Yes, Your Highness," Thantos said with a reluctant bow.

"Maybe you should make a fire, Zephyr," Liz suggested.

"No!" Sir Gallan said. "A fire would only bring unwelcome attention. It is best that we just rest in the dark."

"But, I'm cold," Trinda said.

"No problem, My Lady," Sir Gallan told her.

He removed his red cape and wrapped it around Trinda's shoulders.

So, Zephyr and her friends settled down and rested while the white centaurs and fairy guards kept watch throughout the night. Through Zephyr's mind, thoughts of the oncoming attacks on Crystotopia plagued her, but the soothing sound of the tide coming in and out on the beach helped her get to sleep.

Chapter 5

Brandon's Capture

Early the next morning, Zephyr and her friends prepared to leave. But just as Zephyr was about to mount Tarn, Trinda suddenly screamed.

"Trinda!" Zephyr said as she faced her friend. "What is it?!"

Trinda pointed into the distance, and everyone gasped when he saw what had frightened her.

Emerging from the water were several men moving towards Zephyr and her friends. They had blue hair, gills, and webbed feet, and they were carrying metal tridents as well as wearing blue armor on which the image of a trident was engraved. And, Zephyr could tell that the men didn't seem friendly.

"Vainaquians!" Peantos yelled. "Water wizards to be exact! They are after us!"

Mounting their horses and the white centaurs quickly, Zephyr and her friends tried to flee.

"Follow the coastline to the left!" Little Herb yelled. "That's our only chance for escape!"

Taking off on Tarn, Zephyr galloped away as fast as she could.

However, one of the water wizards screamed quickly, "Aqueous Maximus Executo!"

And, a jet stream of water knocked Brandon off of his horse and onto the sand.

Stopping his own horse, Sir Gallan turned around as he tried to reach Brandon. But another water wizard said, "Waveus Executo!" and a giant wave of water appeared that swept Sir Gallan and his horse backward. Then, the water wizards came upon Brandon.

Standing, Brandon took a defensive fencing stance and began to jab his crystal sword at the water wizards, and as water emerged from his sword, it forced one of the wizards off of his feet.

Next, Brandon clashed his sword with another water wizard's trident. But, the water wizard rotated his trident and pulled back hard, causing Brandon's sword to fly out of his hand.

"No!" Trinda hollered. "Leave him alone!"

Rotating her horse, she charged at the attackers as she shot her sound barrier-breaking arrows to try and ward them off and save Brandon.

One of her arrows hit a water wizard and knocked him down. However, he stood slowly, and he was unharmed due to his armor's protection.

Yet, the sound of Trinda's arrows seemed to affect the water wizards greatly, and they covered their ears to block their high-pitched sounds.

Then, Brandon tried to grab his crystal sword, but he was rendered unconscious as a water wizard whacked him in the back with the blunt end of his trident. Reaching down, the water wizard threw Brandon over his back, and another wizard gripped Brandon's crystal sword.

"Waveus Executo!" a third wizard yelled, and another wave formed that carried the wizards and Brandon into the watery depths of Vainaquia as they vanished from sight.

"No!" Trinda screamed. "They've taken him! They have Brandon!"

Zephyr stared at Trinda with a gaping mouth, for she had never seen her get so upset over another person besides herself before. Usually, she only got angry about her hair getting dirty or from getting too much sun.

"We have to save him!" Trinda said.

"Nay, My Lady," Sir Gallan said. "I'm afraid that is out of the question. We can't forget our mission, and the poor lad has probably been taken straight to King Seadon."

"Zephyr!" Trinda said with tears in her eyes. "Tell him that we have to rescue Brandon! Tell him!"

"Well, I...." Zephyr froze as a memory of the late Prince Toron of Sandus entered her mind.

"No," she said as she shook her head. "It's too dangerous. We have to keep traveling, and it won't help to go rushing into King Seadon's arms. I don't want anyone else to get hurt."

"Oh!" Trinda said angrily. "I refuse to speak to you if you do this Zephyr!"

"Don't get upset," Liz said. "Zephyr's right, Trinda. We have to think of what will work out best."

"You too Liz?!" Trinda said as she turned beat red. "I'm not speaking to either of you then!"

"Let's get going," Little Herb said. "I still have the map of Vainaquia. We should be able to travel by land if we hurry, but we can't stay here any longer. More of King Seadon's men will be here soon."

Though concerned about Brandon, Zephyr and her party began to traverse a small strip of land, which went across Vainaquia. In the back of Zephyr's mind, she wanted to help Brandon, but she forced herself to suppress her feelings and only do what was best for not only her party but Crystotopia as well.

Trinda stared blankly as she rode on her horse and remained very quiet. Sir Gallan had started humming a tune, and Helga couldn't help but shake with fright as she eyed the water around her suspiciously, afraid that something deadly might emerge from it at any second.

But, as the day wore on and the sun rose into the sky, Little Herb warned everyone to pick up his pace.

"We have to move faster!" he said. "If we don't reach Pirates' Cross soon, we won't be able to keep traveling on this strip of land until tomorrow. By high noon, Pirates' Cross will covered by water."

So, everyone began to speed up. However, the sun continued to rise, and the heat of the day was approaching its daily routine temperature. And, Zephyr and her party still had yet to reach what Little Herb called Pirates' Cross.

But then finally, after a couple of hours, Little Herb called out and gave everyone the news that he was glad to hear.

"Pirates' Cross is just ahead!" he yelled.

Peering in front of her, Zephyr saw a rickety wooden bridge swaying in the wind. Though in decay, the condition of the bridge wasn't what worried Zephyr, it was its length.

The sun was already high in the sky, signaling that it was close to noon, and the water around the bridge had elevated so close to it that the crash of the water's waves rattled and wet the bottom of the bridge.

Zephyr and her friends dismounted their horses and the white centaurs as they began to cross the bridge as carefully and as quickly as they could.

Thantos, Peantos, and Reen simply flew across and over the bridge, and they tried to keep it steady for the rest of the party.

"Oh," Helga said nervously. "I don't like this at all, Your Highness. We'd be better off using a flying potion."

"Keep steady!" Sir Gallan said. "And try to move swiftly!"

Suddenly, Tarn's back legs broke through a wooden board on the bridge, making the horse lose her balance.

"Oh, this is the end for me I'm afraid!" Tarn said.

"Relax, Tarn," Zephyr said as she tried to pull her upward. *"Just try and keep going."*

However, just as Zephyr pulled Tarn's legs onto the bridge, the wooden contraption's surface became covered with water, and the water continued to cover more of the bridge each second.

Then, before anyone on the bridge could reach the other side safely, each of them was practically swimming.

"Help!" Zephyr screamed.

Peantos, Reen, and Thantos flew forward and tried to help Zephyr and her friends. But a humongous wave leaped into the air and came crashing down on them and everyone on the bridge, forcing them all into the water.

Zephyr floundered about as the water carried her away. She couldn't see anyone, and when she got her bearings, she swam towards the water's surface.

Emerging from the depths of the salty sea, she gasped as she struggled to breathe.

"Trinda! Helga! Liz!" Zephyr called, but her friends were nowhere to be found, and there was nothing close to Zephyr that she could grab to keep herself afloat.

"Your Highness!" someone suddenly yelled from behind her.

Turning, Zephyr saw the fairy guard Peantos moving in the water, and Zephyr realized that he couldn't fly because his wings were soaking wet.

She peered around herself for something that could help her friends and the rest of her party, but she couldn't even see clearly because of the crashing waves.

Then, she knew that if something wasn't done, she and her friends would perish. But, Zephyr didn't know what to do, and another wave fell over her, dragging her down again. And, as Zephyr forced herself to the surface, she could no longer see Peantos.

Yet, reaching inside herself, Zephyr found the will to help her friends, and if one could see Zephyr's face at this moment, they would notice a look of complete assuredness and that her dangerously brown eyes glittered with light.

"I have to do something," she told herself.

Zephyr closed her eyes and focused while she tried to keep herself afloat, and she spoke loudly.

"As fish swim, and men walk! As fate separates land and water to talk, I command magic to interfere at this cost, or else my party shall be lost! Evolution and adaptation must occur at this time, make my companions wear gills and fins, and breathe like water-bred kind!"

Just as Zephyr said these words, a powerful wave fell on her and pulled her underwater. Zephyr fought to reach the surface again, but she was running out of air.

Then slowly, her eyes closed as she sank. And, the last thing Zephyr heard was a loud fizzling sound.

Chapter 6

King Seadon

M eanwhile, elsewhere in the watery depths of Vainaquia, Brandon Longfellow was dealing with problems of his own.

When he woke up after being knocked out by a water wizard, he was amazed to find that he was slung over the back of the same wizard while he carried him and swam underwater.

Another water wizard was swimming behind the other and was carrying Brandon's crystal sword.

For a second, Brandon was sure that he would drown because he was immersed in water. But, he wasn't gasping for air or struggling to breathe. Then, as he felt his face, he knew why.

Brandon's head was encased in a bubble, which he reasoned had to be magic. He wanted to tell the water wizard that was holding him to let him go, but he didn't say anything for fear of taking in a mouthful of water. And, he didn't even think that the wizard could hear him if he spoke. But, after a second, he thought to himself.

"I can already breathe underwater," he thought. "Maybe I can talk too."

So, Brandon took a chance and spoke.

"Do you think you could put me down?" he asked. "I can swim just fine."

"Well, well," the water wizard carrying him said. "Look who's awake? No, I can't let you go. You're now a prisoner of King Seadon. He'll decide what to do with you."

"Fair enough," Brandon said. "I suppose I couldn't expect it to be any other way. But, if you don't mind my asking, how can I talk to you like this?"

"What!" the wizard said. "Don't tell me you know nothing of magic?! You had a magic crystal sword!"

"I don't know a lot," Brandon said.

"Magic is how you can talk and breathe idiot!" the water wizard said, and his grip on Brandon tightened.

"Everything but the most common sea creatures have spells cast on them to breathe easier and talk to each other underwater! Now, quiet down! The only talking you'll do will be to the King!"

Brandon did keep quiet, but occasionally, he couldn't help but gasp at the things he saw in Vainaquia, and it made him wonder if he wanted to live underwater.

He observed various schools of different colored fish, lobsters, crabs, and shrimp. There were many cave dwellings made of stone and coral on the sea floor, in which water wizards and witches seemed to live. Also, there were even outdoor stores, which were selling fish and other types of seafood in exchange for other items.

Brandon also saw several water wizards and witches riding seahorses. He passed jellyfish and killer whales, and as he went even deeper into the sea, he came across mermaids and mermen. (They all seemed extremely curious about Brandon, though the water wizards escorting him kept chasing them away).

Then soon, Brandon came across coral reefs, crevices filled with bubbles, abandoned ships, and underwater volcanoes and hot spots.

He was starting to think that the wondrous underwater realm was never-ending.

But, though Brandon saw a great deal, he wasn't prepared for an underwater city or King Seadon's castle, and he knew what they both were as soon as he saw them.

Eventually, the water wizards escorting him approached a giant dome structure and a huge pair of gates made of sapphire that led inside it.

As Brandon moved closer to the dome structure, the gates were opened, and within, there was a city of immense beauty with sapphire houses everywhere.

"This is the capital city of Vainaquia," one of the water wizards told Brandon. "It is called Currentia."

Brandon noticed an assortment of underwater beings frolicking about almost as if they were on land. However, he also noticed that the entire city was full of carefully placed mirrors, which the citizens constantly looked into. There were even people gazing into personal hand mirrors while trying on jewelry and different clothing. And, as beautiful as the city seemed, everyone only paid attention to his own appearance.

Then, in the center of the city, there stood a castle made of sapphire that sparkled almost as much as the Crystal Castle in Crystotopia, and Brandon gulped as he was led inside it.

The water wizards took Brandon down a series of corridors until they emerged from a pool of water and into what Brandon guessed was a throne room. And, Brandon was tossed to the ground.

Shockingly, however, the throne room wasn't underwater, though Brandon barely had a chance to look around before he was forced to bow.

The entire throne room was just as full of huge wall mirrors as it was of guards. And, sitting on a large golden and sapphire throne, was the biggest whale Brandon had ever seen.

The whale was male, and he possessed eyes that were a vivid sparkling blue that seemed as deep as the sea, and he had skin that was both white and gray. He wore blue robes and a giant golden crown. Also, though Brandon couldn't tell which it was, in his right hand or fin, the whale held a sparkling sapphire blue trident. And, at the bottom of the whale's tail, there sat a small pool of water, which he slipped his fins into and out of on a routine basis.

Two water witches stood on opposite sides of the whale and held large mirrors up so he could look at himself.

"Oh fair and great King Seadon," the water wizard that had captured Brandon said as he bowed. "We have brought you a prisoner. He was found resting on the edge of your vast and magnificent kingdom, and we think he is a traveler from Crystotopia."

"Really?" the giant whale said in a booming voice.

"What were you doing in such an interesting place, boy?" he asked.

"You see...." Brandon said in a nervous tone.

He had never seen a talking whale before or a whale quite as big as this one.

"Go on!" Seadon commanded.

"Speak boy!" a water wizard told Brandon as he hit him in the back of his head. Unbelievably, the bubble around Brandon's head didn't burst as he was hit, and he felt the full magnitude of the pain from the water wizard's hand.

"I was just...passing through," he said.

"Liar!" one of the water wizards said.

He picked Brandon up and slapped him hard. "Tell the truth!"

"Wait!" Seadon said suddenly. "Come here, young man."

Standing, Brandon faced King Seadon, but he was afraid that if he approached the whale, he might swallow him whole.

"I said come here!" Seadon said.

He pointed his trident at Brandon, and a stream of water swept underneath him and carried him in front of Seadon. Then, the Whale King put his fin under Brandon's face and lifted it carefully.

"Yes, I see," he said. "My dear boy, I think your face is perfectly symmetrical. You know, you are quite handsome. I saw it just now as my guard smacked you."

"Excuse me?" Brandon said.

"Azure, Wild Wave, adjust the mirrors to reflect this young man's handsome features," King Seadon said.

The two water witches standing beside him holding up mirrors, adjusted them to reflect Brandon's face.

"Amazing," Seadon said. "The flatness of your nose, the curliness of your hair. Why, you could pass for my son."

"I could?!" Brandon said with disbelief. "But, I don't look like a...a whale."

"Is that to say you think yourself more handsome than I?!" Seadon asked as he pointed his trident at Brandon in a threatening manner.

"Of course not, Your Majesty," Brandon said as he held up his hands and backed away. "What I mean to say is that my features can't compare to yours. Why just look at your massive uh...fins. They are extraordinary!"

"Yes," Seadon said. "They are quite the sight, aren't they? I keep them trim and fit."

"Yes, and your eyes," Brandon said. "They are so...so blue."

Secretly, Brandon was ready to puke at every compliment he gave to King Seadon.

"Of course," Seadon said. "They are sometimes my best feature. Azure, Wild Wave, the mirrors! Quickly!"

The water witches placed the mirrors they held in front of Seadon once more. "Hmm," he said as he peered into the mirrors. "I can see what you mean. I am quite attractive. Why, there isn't anyone in this kingdom who matches my appearance."

"Sire," a water wizard said as he cleared his throat. "May I bring it to your attention that this boy was trespassing and may be in league with Crystotopia and King Lionus?"

"Lionus!" Seadon said loudly. His voice was so strong that it shook the throne room. "How I do hate that fellow! He and his land-dwelling crystal miners think themselves more attractive than I! But, I am the most handsome being in all of Danus! At least my people know the truth. That Lionus and that late wife of his pale in comparison to me!"

"But perhaps, oh wise and noble King," the water wizard said. "You should check to see where this boy is from. You said to yourself that he is attractive. What if he thinks himself more handsome than you or even Lionus?"

"Yes," Seadon said. "Where are you from boy, and what is your name?"

"My name is Brandon Longfellow," Brandon said. "And I'm not from Crystotopia. I'm from Earth."

"Earth...earth," Seadon mumbled. "Now, where have I heard of that place before?"

"No matter," he said as he pointed his trident at Brandon. "I don't need to ask questions to find out what I need to know. I can see for myself."

A black beam of light shot forward from Seadon's trident and hit Brandon in the stomach, and Brandon fell forward in shock. He was in such immense pain that he couldn't even speak.

Then, a black sphere of light flew from him and settled into the pool of water at King Seadon's feet as swirling images appeared within it.

Brandon could see pictures of several things that resembled events that had happened in his past.

Then, King Seadon roared and splashed the pool of water with his trident as soon as he saw the Crystal Castle.

"So!" he bellowed. "You are helping Crystotopia, and you are in cahoots with that ugly scoundrel, Lionus, and his daughter! Crystotopia is our greatest enemy! Why, you probably came here to pretend to be an ally and trick my subjects into thinking that you are as handsome as I! I am the fairest in the land, you hear me! And, after tomorrow, there will be no question of it! For, you will be beheaded at dawn!"

"No!" Brandon said with a gasp.

"And soon!" Seadon said. "Crystotopia shall fall at the hands of the Dark Forces as well! Guards, throw this boy in the dungeon, and don't treat him with even the slightest ounce of respect! To think that I thought of you as a son!"

The guards approached Brandon, but just as they grabbed him, something emerged from the water at the throne room entrance.

Turning his head, Brandon's eyes widened with awe as he saw a giant whale almost as big as King Seadon. This whale even had blue eyes just like the King's, but it was a female, and she wore a bouquet of coral on her head.

"Hello," the whale said with a giddy laugh.

"Ah, my beautiful daughter, Princess Tidea," King Seadon said. "What do we owe the pleasure of your visit, a gracious creature whose beauty is surpassed only by my own?"

"Oh," Tidea said. "I've just heard that a new prisoner has been captured, and I had to see him for myself."

"Here he is," King Seadon said as he aimed his trident at Brandon. "In league with Crystotopia. Brandon Longfellow is his name, and he is to be beheaded in the morning."

As Brandon was pulled towards the throne room entrance by two water wizards, Princess Tidea took his face and held it up to her eyes.

"Father!" she said excitedly. "Why, he's just gorgeous! I've never seen anyone quite like him, and his features are stunning!"

"Yes," King Seadon said. "But of course, they don't compare to ours, dearest daughter."

"Oh I know," Tidea said. "But I've been looking for a new husband. Do you suppose I can marry this one? I'd love to have him."

"You may have his head in the morning," Seadon said.

"Come now, father. I want all of him."

Princess Tidea squeezed Brandon so tightly that his face turned blue.

"No, daughter," King Seadon said. "He is a traitor, and he thinks himself better looking than me."

"Oh no, Your Majesty," Brandon said between deep breaths. "You and your daughter are the loveliest whales I've ever laid eyes on. Honest."

"My, my," Princess Tidea said with a giggle. "Flattery will get you everywhere. You're very charming."

She walked over to the water wizard who was carrying Brandon's crystal sword and snatched it with her fin as the sword began to glow blue in her grasp.

"Look father!" she said as she waved the sword in the air and splashed water in different directions. "It's a crystal sword, and it's almost like your trident when I hold it. This would make a nice wedding present."

"Very well," King Seadon said with a sigh. "You may have him as your next husband Tidea, and you may marry him in the morning."

"Thank you, Father," Princess Tidea said in a sweet voice.

Then, she narrowed her eyes at the water wizards in the throne room.

"Guards!" she screamed. "Take the prisoner and prepare him for tomorrow's wedding!"

"You do wish to marry my beautiful daughter do you not?" King Seadon asked Brandon.

"Of course," Brandon said with a gulp. "I'd love to marry her."

And then, the guards took Brandon away.

"How bad could marriage be anyway?" Brandon said as he was led out of the throne room. "She is a princess after all, and it's much better than being beheaded."

"Ha!" one of the guards said. "That's what you think! Princess Tidea has a new husband every month because she always ends up wondering what her husbands taste like! She'll eat you soon enough, and you'll practically be a slave to her until she does it!"

"Great!" Brandon said under his breath.

And, he remained speechless as King Seadon's guards took him away. But, even if he could think of something to say, he knew it wouldn't be pleasant. However, all Brandon pondered on was marriage and the end of his life.

Chapter 7

Princess Tidea's Wedding

Deep in the midst of Vainaquia, Zephyr and her party lay beneath the waves. But they were all in disbelief, for apparently, they had been transformed into sea creatures.

Zephyr, Elizabeth, Trinda, and Helga were mermaids, and Sir Gallan and Little Herb were mermen. The horses had become large seahorses with gills, fins, and curved tails. And, the white centaurs, Trion, Valon, Piro, and Cara were now part seahorse and part person.

However, the strangest case was that of the fairy guards, Thantos, Reen, and Peantos, for they had been turned into creatures that looked like seals, and their wings had become webbed flippers.

"What happened?!" Zephyr screamed as she examined her new iridescent green tail. Touching it, she gasped when she found that it was also sleek and scaly.

"What happened to me?!" she yelled in a frantic tone. "To us?!"

"Stop that!" Elizabeth said as she shook Zephyr to her senses. "Why are you screaming?! You're the one who cast the spell!"

"I cast the spell?" Zephyr said with awe. "I turned us into this?!"

"Correct!" Liz said. "And I would have done the same if I were you."

Though Zephyr couldn't believe what she had done, she tried to accept the fact that she had transformed her and her friends with magic. But she wasn't the only one in shock.

"How did you do this?!" Peantos asked anxiously. "I'm a fairy, and my wings are gone!"

"Too late to think about that now," Little Herb said. "We have to keep traveling! We're still in dangerous territory you know."

"But I can't," Zephyr said as she gawked at her tail. "I don't have the slightest idea about how to swim with this thing!"

"Oh it's easy," Liz said as she swam circles around Zephyr. "Just try it. It's almost like regular swimming but even simpler."

Zephyr tried to move her tail, and after a few minutes, she found herself swimming whichever way she chose.

"This is much more fun than walking!" she said.

"It's only temporary I hope," Sir Gallan said.

"Maybe we can find Brandon while we're down here!" Trinda said.

"We might come across him," Zephyr said. "Which way do we go, Little Herb?"

"I can't tell," Little Herb said. "The map has been damaged by the water."

"Let's just try and find our way without the map," Sir Gallan said. "We can't stay here."

As they mounted the seahorses and the newly transformed white centaurs, Zephyr and her party took off as they swam through the sea.

"This is so strange," Tarn told Zephyr. *"It's somewhat scary but swimming like a seahorse seems so natural."*

"I know what you mean Tarn," Zephyr said with a laugh.

Together, Zephyr and her friends swam for what seemed like ages, and they passed by many Vainaquians and water creatures. And fortunately, no one realized that Zephyr and her friends were from Crystotopia. Disguised and turned into water-dwelling creatures, they were inconspicuous.

However, the further they delved into the kingdom, the more lost they became, and Little Herb finally stopped and threw his hands up in frustration.

"Okay!" he said. "We are officially lost!"

"Lost?" Sir Gallan said. "If we don't make it to Aeria, our quest will be in vain."

"Perhaps we should split up," Trion suggested.

"No," Sir Gallan said. "Our best chance for success is to stay together."

"Well, what should we do?" Zephyr asked as she glanced at Elizabeth.

"For once, Zephyr," Liz said slowly. "I don't have any ideas. You'll have to ask someone else."

Zephyr lowered her head sadly, but just then, a large school of rainbow trout passed above her head.

"You're right, Liz," Zephyr said with a smirk. "That's just what I'll do!"

Dismounting Tarn and swimming forward, Zephyr spoke to the school of fish.

"Excuse me!" she said. *"Excuse me!"*

"Out of our way, mermaid!" one of the larger trout said. *"We don't have time to talk to you!"*

"Well that's just plain rude," Zephyr said as she put her hands on her hips. *"All I need are directions. It will only take a minute."*

"Maybe we should help the pretty mermaid," a smaller and obviously younger fish suggested.

"No!" a larger trout said. *"We shouldn't pay any attention to some silly mermaid! They only talk about how pretty they are! That's all she probably really wants to know! Besides, I've never heard of a mermaid that needed directions in Vainaquia in my life!"*

"But, I do need directions," Zephyr said. *"Please, I'm really lost, and I'm not actually a mermaid anyway."*

"Oh!" another small trout said. *"That is something! What are you?!"*

"I'm a sorceress," Zephyr said.

"Wow!" several smaller fish said.

They broke away from the school of fish and swam around Zephyr excitedly.

"I've never seen a sorceress before!" the smallest trout said.

"Well, I have!" the biggest of the trout said. *"And it sounds quite suspicious to me! But that might explain why she can talk to us! Most Vainaquians can't! Come along children! We can't waste another second! We are in a hurry! Simply leave this stranger be! She probably means trouble, and why, she might even be from Crystotopia or Aeria! Those wretched kingdoms!"*

"But I only need...." Zephyr started to say.

"That's quite enough!" the biggest fish said loudly as he waved his fin in Zephyr's face. *"As I said before, we are in a hurry! Good day!"*

"Can you at least tell me where I can get help from?" Zephyr asked.

"Probably nowhere," one of the larger trout said as he swam away. *"Everyone is going to be at Princess Tidea's wedding. She's to marry her fiftieth husband at dawn, and King Seadon has sent word throughout the entire kingdom. The groom is supposed to be one of the most handsome yet."*

"King Seadon," Zephyr said under her breath.

Then, she swam back to her party.

"Those fish said something about a wedding," she told them. "A princess is getting married. And, if we follow them, I think they will lead us to King Seadon and hopefully, Brandon."

"We can't go there!" Sir Gallan said. "We want to get to Aeria and avoid King Seadon!"

"I think we should follow them," Trinda said. "We can't let Brandon stay with that king! I shudder to think of the horrors he may be facing!"

"We have to go that way anyway," Zephyr said. "One of those trout told me that the whole kingdom is going to attend the wedding. Our best chance of finding a way out of Vainaquia is to follow them."

"I think we can take our chances and find our way out of this place on our own," Helga said fearfully. "Does this King Seadon like to eat dwarves?"

"Come on," Zephyr said. "The fish are swimming away. We have to catch up."

"Oh, I knew you were going to say that, Your Highness," Helga said with a sigh. Together, Zephyr and her friends took off after the school of rainbow trout, and the brave party trailed the fish for hours.

Trinda kept asking in a painfully annoying voice, "Are we going the right way?" or "How much further is it?"

Eventually, Zephyr and her party came across an assortment of other sea creatures including water wizards and witches as well as mermaids and mermen who all seemed to be going to Princess Tidea's wedding. Unfortunately, whenever Zephyr asked someone for directions leading to Aeria, everyone would say that he was in a hurry. So, Zephyr was starting to think that she should ask the princess herself for directions.

Then finally, Zephyr and her friends reached the site of the wedding, and they felt they should be exhausted for they had traveled all day and night.

Amazingly, however, they weren't extremely tired or drowsy, which was most likely a positive characteristic of their current physical states.

Just ahead, piles of various Vainaquians poured into what seemed to be sapphire gates leading into a city. And of course, although Zephyr and her companions didn't know it, this was Currentia, the same city where Brandon had been taken by a group of water wizards.

Guards were posted everywhere, and Zephyr was weary of them, but she was determined to enter the city anyway.

"Your Highness, wait!" Sir Gallan said as he stopped Zephyr, Liz, and Tarn. "We can't go in there! We'll be surrounded by King Seadon and his men!"

"We have to get directions from somebody," Zephyr said. "We need to find someone who is polite enough to take five minutes to give us some, and they won't be able to tell who we are anyway."

"Perhaps we should listen to Sir Gallan, Your Highness," Peantos said. "Your safety is an issue."

"Oh!" Trinda said angrily. "You men are so useless! Brandon needs us, and none of the women here are afraid to go in there!"

"I'm scared!" Helga said quickly.

But Zephyr led Tarn forward anyway, and her companions followed her. Zephyr eyed the guards around her nervously as she swam through the gates of Currentia, but they didn't seem to be suspicious of her identity.

As Trinda entered the city, she sighed with delight as she caught sight of the abundance of mirrors placed everywhere. Swimming forward, she moved over to a large mirror and posed in front of it.

"Wow!" she said happily. "I look absolutely gorgeous with this tail, and I'm probably the most beautiful mermaid around!"

"And just who do you think you are?!" an orange-haired mermaid behind Trinda asked her. "Black hair is out honey!"

"Orange is the new color of choice," she said as she primped her hair. "Don't you think?!"

Zephyr held her breath just as the orange-haired mermaid spoke, for she knew that no one in her right mind would challenge Trinda Temple's beauty.

Darting her golden eyes at the mermaid behind her, Trinda pulled on her orange hair and she started to talk to her through clenched teeth.

"You aren't as 'in' as you think!" she said. "You should know, gentlemen prefer blacks!"

"Ow!" the orange-haired mermaid said.

With a heavy shove, Trinda released her, and the mermaid swam away as she glared at Trinda reproachfully.

Hag!" she yelled.

Zephyr giggled softly at Trinda's skirmish, and interestingly most Vainaquians paid attention to her. Trinda got compliments from several people as she and the rest of Zephyr's party moved through Currentia. And, Zephyr and Liz had to keep pulling Trinda away from the mirrors stationed around the city.

When Zephyr and her friends drew nearer to King Seadon's castle, they found that a crowd of Vainaquians surrounded the castle entrance as well as a long gold and sapphire walkway, which extended from it, and Zephyr knew they were waiting for the wedding to take place.

Zephyr and her friends settled into the crowd, and Zephyr thought that because everyone who was in a hurry had at last reached the site of Princess Tidea's wedding it was safe to ask for directions.

"Excuse me!" she said to a brown-haired merman as she tapped him on the shoulder. "Do you think you could give me directions?"

However, the merman turned and shot her an evil look.

"Can't you see that a wedding is about to happen?!" he said angrily.

"Sorry," Zephyr said.

"No one will help us," she told her friends with a sigh. "It's no good asking."

"You just have to know 'how' to ask," Trinda said.

She tapped the same merman on the shoulder that Zephyr had just spoken to.

"I thought I told you...." the merman said as he turned hastily.

However, he froze as he stared at Trinda while she batted her golden eyes.

"Oh," he said nervously. "I thought you were someone else. What can I do for you?"

"Well," Trinda said as she threw up her hand in a helpless manner. "I just can't seem to find my way to Aeria. I'm trying to move in that direction because I hear that...um...that the edge of Vainaquia is prime real estate."

"Not even," the merman said. "No place is better than Currentia, especially for a mer-maid-like you."

"No, no," Trinda said with a laugh. "I'm definitely interested in the section of Vainaquia near Aeria, and I'm sure that such a strong and handsome guy like you can help me out."

"Of course," the merman answered.

But just as he was about to tell Trinda exactly what she wanted to hear, coral trumpets sounded, and the entire crowd of people floated quietly and stared with eager eyes at the castle entrance.

"Presenting, His Majesty, King Seadon of Vainaquia!" a water wizard announced, and Zephyr guessed that the water wizard was a herald.

Then, King Seadon came out of the castle entrance holding his sapphire blue trident along with a merman dressed in lavish blue and golden clothing.

Zephyr, Liz, and Trinda gasped at the sight of King Seadon, for just like Brandon, they had never seen a giant whale.

The merman next to the King moved behind him, and he was carrying a book with laminated pages of parchment that possessed the image of a trident on its cover.

Slowly, the King and the merman swam to the edge of the walkway, and the crowd of people 'ohhed' and 'ahhed' as they looked at the King with admiration.

"This isn't a good idea, Your Highness," Helga told Zephyr.

"Stay calm," Zephyr whispered.

"I'm guessing that merman is kind of like a priest," Liz whispered.

"Fair people of Vainaquia," King Seadon said in a loud voice. "Today is a very special occasion. My fair daughter, Princess Tidea, second only to my attractiveness, has chosen her fiftieth husband. This is truly an important event, for this husband is no mere Vainaquian. He is a land dweller with very unique and handsome features."

As the King spoke, the crowd talked amongst themselves in excited whispers.

"Who wants to marry someone who has had that many husbands?" Trinda asked quietly.

"May I introduce, the groom, Brandon Longfellow!" King Seadon said, and Trinda nearly fainted.

"What!" she yelled. "How dare...."

Before Trinda could make another sound, Zephyr and Liz covered her mouth and held her down.

Then, King Seadon motioned to the castle entrance, and the crowd waited. However, Brandon didn't show up.

"He's just a little shy," King Seadon said with a laugh.

The King pointed his trident at the castle entrance, and Brandon was carried outside by a current of water, which stopped in front of Seadon.

Brandon was also dressed in lavish blue and gold attire, though the ball and chain attached to his foot, and the shackles on his arms seemed out of place for a wedding.

But, upon Brandon's debut, the crowd cheered and watched him with marvel.

"There we are my boy," King Seadon whispered to Brandon. "You're very lucky."

"I don't want to marry...." Brandon was about to say.

However, he couldn't find the courage to finish speaking because King Seadon held his trident at Brandon's throat and glared at him.

"They're forcing Brandon to marry the Princess," Elizabeth whispered with amazement.

"Yes," Zephyr said.

Turning, she faced Sir Gallan.

"We have to save Brandon," she told him in a low voice.

"We can't," Sir Gallan said. "That's a very weak strategy. We would never get out of here alive."

"We can't leave him," Zephyr said. "If you don't do anything, I will."

"Fine," Sir Gallan said with a sigh as he shook his head. "If you absolutely insist. First, we need to let Brandon know that we are here without giving ourselves away or exciting him."

"Let me try," Trinda said eagerly, and she shook her jet-black curls as she eyed Brandon.

"Wow!" she bellowed suddenly. "That Brandon Longfellow is so good-looking. I wish I could marry him instead of him marrying Princess Tidea!"

As she spoke, Brandon saw Trinda immediately and beamed with hope, but Trinda got more attention than she bargained for as the entire crowd of people stared at her. And surprisingly, there were gasps and sounds made as people took notice of her appearance.

"Amazing!" one merman said. "She's hot! Maybe she 'should' marry that Brandon fellow!"

"I don't know what sea rock she climbed from under," a mermaid said with envy. "She probably looks terrible in the morning."

"Why, she's even more attractive than Princess Tidea," an old mermaid said.

"Trinda!" Brandon called happily, and King Seadon eyed both him and Trinda suspiciously.

"Silence!" he screamed, and everyone grew deathly quiet, for King Seadon seemed to be in a frightfully bad mood.

"Who is this girl?!" he said.

"Do you know the groom young mermaid?" he asked Trinda.

"Uh well...." Trinda started to say as she smiled anxiously.

But, she couldn't think of what to say next, and she was overwhelmed that she was talking to King Seadon.

"I've met her before!" Brandon said quickly. "I did...did some vacationing in Vainaquia, and we ran into each other."

"Oh," King Seadon said. "That makes sense. She is quite an attractive mermaid, and it is possible that your paths crossed before."

"Are you engaged, my dear?" King Seadon asked Trinda.

"I...I..." Trinda mumbled.

"Sire!" one of the guards said suddenly. "The wedding!"

"Yes, yes," King Seadon said. "Carry on."

An orchestra of underwater beings started to play wedding music on a plethora of colorful shells that had been shaped into instruments, and more coral trumpets sounded.

"Presenting Her Highness, the beautiful, Princess Tidea!" the herald announced.

The whale Princess swam through the castle entrance, wearing a blue dress and carrying a bouquet of seaweed in her hand.

Behind her, a water wizard walked as he held a blue pillow on which, Zephyr noticed that Brandon's crystal sword rested.

"Oh my," Princess Tidea said in a giddy voice. "This is all so wonderful! I've forgotten how touching weddings are, well since my last one anyway."

"Your Highness," Sir Gallan whispered to Zephyr. "Perhaps you should use some magic. I think it is the best solution."

"I think so too," Zephyr said.

But, as she observed the heavy amount of security around her, she didn't think any spell she could cast would lead to a successful venture.

"Hear ye, hear ye," the priest-like merman said.

Opening the laminated book he held, he started to read from it out loud.

"We are gathered here today to celebrate the union of Princess Tidea and her newest groom, Brandon Longfellow."

Gulping, Brandon eyed Trinda. However, his gaze was so intense that it caught Princess Tidea's attention.

"No! No!" Princess Tidea said. "Stop the wedding! What are you looking at Brandon?! Your eyes should be focused on me, and this wedding must be perfect!" Turning, Princess Tidea spotted Trinda, and the Princess' deep blue eyes narrowed with malicious intentions.

"Wait!" she shouted. "Who is that?!"

"What's the matter, dear?" King Seadon asked.

"That mermaid!" Princess Tidea bellowed as she pointed at Trinda. "I've never seen a mermaid look like that, and it seems that Brandon fancies staring at her instead of me!"

"I'm the most beautiful in the land, second only to you father!" Princess Tidea yelled as she swam up and down with rage.

"I'll show her what happens to little mermaids that think they can beat me, Princess Tidea!"

"Yes," King Seadon said. "She is quite attractive, but you should pay attention to the wedding dear. The mermaid is no threat!"

But the Princess ignored her father.

"Guards!" she shouted. "Seize that girl! I don't like the way my husband watches her, and no mermaid can match my beauty!"

"Zephyr now!" Sir Gallan shouted.

"Everyone, cover your eyes!" Zephyr yelled to her party, and all of Zephyr's friends including Brandon obeyed her instructions.

Thinking, "Lightnus Maximus Executo!" Zephyr waved her hand.

And, a blinding light engulfed the people of Currentia, and screams echoed throughout the city.

However, King Seadon whirled his trident, and a black light flashed that made the blinding light subside.

"Father!" Princess Tidea yelled in a whining voice. "They are escaping with my husband!"

"They've even taken my wedding present!" she screamed as she pointed to the blue pillow that the water wizard held behind her head, and King Seadon saw that Brandon's crystal sword was gone. Also, the shackles and the ball and chain that held Brandon had been cut and left on the castle walkway.

Then, Princess Tidea nodded towards the entrance of Currentia, and King Seadon noticed that Zephyr and her party were swimming away with Brandon in Sir Gallan's arms, and Brandon was holding his crystal sword.

"How dare they!" King Seadon roared. "No one will make a fool of me and my daughter!"

Angered, King Seadon took off after Zephyr's party at amazing speed with his trident in hand.

"We still don't know which way to go," Zephyr said once she and her friends made it out of the city gates.

"Go for the surface!" Sir Gallan said. "You'll never make it in the water! King Seadon will kill us first! Go! I will try to hold him back!"

Placing Brandon on Valon's back, Sir Gallan unsheathed his long broad sword as he faced King Seadon.

"Zephyr!" Liz called. "You have to undo your spell! Turn us back into our old selves, or else we won't be able to survive on land!"

"But, I don't know how to!" Zephyr said.

"Well, you better do something!" Trinda said. "Our other options aren't looking so good!"

"But I...." Zephyr started to say.

However, as she saw the giant form of King Seadon speeding towards her and her friends, she knew that Liz and Trinda were right.

"Okay," she said. "I'll do my best!"

Yet, just as Zephyr raised her hands to cast her spell, King Seadon's magnified roar broke her concentration.

Peering down, she watched in fear as the Whale King broke through Currentia's entrance, knocking the sapphire gates off of their hinges.

Swimming to the left, Sir Gallan managed to dodge Seadon's attempt to swallow him, and he sideswiped the King as he hit him on the side with the hilt of his sword.

But as King Seadon rotated and charged at Sir Gallan again, he aimed his trident at the Ruby Knight. A black beam of light shot toward him, and upon impact, Sir Gallan flipped backward into the water as he stopped moving.

"No!" Zephyr shouted.

"He needs my help!" Brandon yelled as he narrowed his eyes boldly.

"Zephyr!" he said. "Finish your spell! I'll help Sir Gallan!"

"Brandon wait!" Trinda screamed, but Brandon had already jumped off of Valon's back as he swam towards King Seadon and Sir Gallan.

As fast as he could, the Whale King was charging at Sir Gallan's motionless body, but just before he ate the Ruby Knight whole, a powerful jet stream of water pushed him to the sea floor.

Looking up and roaring, Seadon seemed to shake all of Vainaquia as he glared at Brandon and his crystal sword.

"So!" he said. "This is the thanks I get for almost making you a part of my family!"

"Ha!" Brandon said. "Some family! I'd rather have my tongue cut off than marry your daughter!"

"That can be arranged!" King Seadon yelled.

Then, raising his trident at Brandon, he produced a whirlwind of water that flew at him.

Brandon tried to hold his crystal sword up for defense, but he was knocked against a rocky wall by Seadon's magic.

Coming to his senses, Sir Gallan took a battle stance as he faced King Seadon.

But, the Whale King created a wave of black light that flew at Brandon, and Brandon barely moved out of the way before the rocky wall he was against blew to pieces, and he was tossed through the water by the might of the explosion.

Just as Brandon started to get his bearings, King Seadon was almost upon him, but Sir Gallan swept Brandon away and carried him to safety.

"This isn't your fight lad!" Sir Gallan said. "Save yourself!"

"You need my help!" Brandon said. "Admit it!"

Yet, before Sir Gallan could answer, he faced King Seadon as he was almost upon him and Brandon.

"You should be dead by now!" King Seadon told Sir Gallan.

"Really?!" Sir Gallan said. "Haven't you heard of magical armor, Seadon?!"

"You may have escaped me once!" Seadon screamed. "But you will not be so lucky again!"

Just as King Seadon reached Sir Gallan, he clashed his trident against the Ruby Knight's sword.

"Hurry, Zephyr!" Liz said. "Don't just float there and watch!"

Shaking her head, Zephyr stopped staring at Sir Gallan and Brandon as she closed her eyes and raised her hands.

"Though we swim, it was just a whim! What saved us then, must come to an end! Magic I call, to help us withdraw! Reverse the spell, and make us ourselves!"

As Zephyr said the words of her incantation, she and her party swam to the surface and emerged from the depths of the water.

However, a heavy fog was in the air and very little could be seen. Zephyr's spell had yet to work, and land was nowhere in sight. Also, Sir Gallan and Brandon were still underwater fighting with King Seadon.

"We're in the middle of the sea," Zephyr said. "Which way do we go, Little Herb?"

"I have no idea," the healer said as he shook his head.

"We're doomed, Your Highness!" Helga said as she cringed with fear.

But suddenly, there was a loud fizzing sound, and a gray light surrounded Zephyr and her friends.

Then, after a moment, they were restored to their former selves and were wearing their old clothes.

"Help, Your Highness!" Helga yelled as she floundered about in the water. "I can't swim!"

Grabbing Helga, Zephyr tried to help her stay afloat, but she was preparing for the worst. As she and her friends sat in the middle of the sea, the overwhelming vastness of it seemed hopeless for them to overcome, and Peantos, Thantos, and Reen still couldn't fly because their wings were wet.

But upon Zephyr giving up hope, a humongous wooden ship revealed itself in the midst of the fog.

"Help!" Zephyr yelled as she waved her hands at the ship. "Help us please!"

"Save us!" Trinda hollered.

"Yes!" Liz said.

Zephyr couldn't make out what anyone on the ship looked like because of the fog, but she and her party tried to get the crew's attention regardless of that fact.

Then, an anchor dropped into the water, and ropes and nets were thrown down as the crew helped Zephyr and her friends onto the ship.

However, it took an abundance of ropes and nets to get the white centaurs and Tarn and the other horses onto the ship as well.

"Is that the whole lot of you?" someone asked.

"No," Zephyr said. "There are two more!"

She peered into the fog and over the ship with worried eyes.

"They must be gone by now, Your Highness," Piro said. "Brandon and Sir Gallan have been under the water too long. King Seadon must have gotten to them."

Yet, as Piro spoke, a giant whirlwind of water emerged from the sea, and everyone could hear Brandon and Sir Gallan yelling.

Then, with a heavy thud, they both landed on the deck of the ship, soaking wet and with their weapons, and Zephyr saw that the magic bubble encased around Brandon's head had been destroyed.

"Oh, you two are safe!" Trinda said happily as she ran to hug Brandon and Sir Gallan.

"Ah fair maiden," Sir Gallan said as he tried to get his breath. "It is nothing really. I am fine."

"I don't...think King Seadon wants me to be his son, anymore," Brandon said as he coughed, and Trinda laughed.

However, Sir Gallan moaned as he tried to sit up and stand.

"Are you injured?" Little Herb asked as he ran to the Ruby Knight's side.

"Not now!" Sir Gallan said. "We must get away from here! King Seadon is bound to come after us!"

"Right men!" one of the ship's crewmembers said. "All hands on deck! The Sea King is in a foul mood!"

However, Zephyr was a little concerned because she still couldn't see any of the ship's crew clearly, let alone her friends.

"Excuse me?" she said to one of the members. "Who are you exactly? I haven't properly thanked you for saving us! Please, let us know what we can do to repay you."

"Oh, I wouldn't worry about that too much lass," the crewmember replied. "Or should I say, Your Highness, like your white centaur friend? Repay us you will. You and your friends should catch a pretty penny or two. You're all now captives of Captain White Beard!"

Then, a smelly and hideous man unmasked himself to Zephyr as he moved closer to her. With dirty charcoal skin, a long white beard, one brown eye showing and a black eye patch covering the other, wearing red and white robes, possessing rotted teeth and a dagger and fancy cutlass at his side, Zephyr realized that the man she was speaking to was a pirate and Captain White Beard himself.

"What...." Zephyr started to say.

But before any of her friends knew what was happening, they were disarmed and tied up.

Then, as the ship moved and the fog encircling it dissipated, everyone in Zephyr's party could see that he was on a pirate ship that carried a signature black flag bearing a skull and crossbones.

Also, the crew of the ship were some of the ugliest, dirtiest, and most disgusting men Zephyr had ever seen complete with terrible manners, nasty wicked laughs, and horrible dispositions.

Even still, Zephyr and her friends had yet to escape from King Seadon's grasp. For, as the pirate ship sailed off, thunder sounded, storm clouds circled in the sky, and massive waves came from all directions as a tempest formed itself.

"Argh!" Captain White Beard said. "You've really gotten the Sea King mad! I've never seen a storm quite like this!"

Then suddenly, winds started to howl, and whirlpools appeared in the sea.

"I think I'm going to be sick!" Helga said, and she struggled to keep from hurling.

"This isn't good," Brandon said. "King Seadon will kill us for sure!"

"Fear not boy!" Captain White Beard said. "We'll make sure you reach the slave market! We pirates know how to deal with the King's wrath. This is a magic ship." Captain White Beard walked over to the center of the ship and pulled a lever. Then, there was a clanking sound of wheels turning as wooden and parchment wings slipped out from the ship's sides and began to flap.

"Air magic from our business associates in Aeria," Captain White Beard said with a laugh.

Slowly, Zephyr watched in awe as Captain White Beard's ship took off into the sky.

Just as the ship started to rise, an enraged King Seadon emerged from the water and leaped into the air. Luckily, he missed the ship by the length of a small hair, and it eventually flew away from the reach and influence of King Seadon and his magical trident's powers.

Soon, Captain White Beard's ship was high in the clouds where the sun shone brighter than ever, and the ship sailed through the skies with ease.

But although Zephyr and her party had managed to flee from King Seadon and Brandon's marriage to Princess Tidea, it was no time to rejoice. For now, they had to confront Captain White Beard and his band of pirates, and Zephyr wasn't sure if that was better or worse than dealing with their previous predicament. And, in Brandon's words, "They were out of a bind and in another."

Chapter 8

The Great Stair

"This is it, Your Highness," Helga said with a whimper. "I have to say my final words. I realize that I'll never see my parents or Gusto again. You're the only witness to my last will and testament."

"Helga please," Zephyr said irritably. "You're not going to die."

"Unfortunately, Your Highness," Captain White Beard said. "That's up to your new master. I don't care what he does with you once he gets you. But, I have to deliver you in good condition."

"My father will have your head when he finds out what you've done!" Zephyr said.

"Ha!" Captain White Beard laughed. "Silly, Princess. Everyone knows that Crystotopia is about to be taken over by the Dark Forces. Without his sword, your father won't last long in battle. Why, the battle's probably over right now."

While Captain White Beard spoke, his crew rummaged through all of Zephyr and her friends' things, and they had discovered through reasoning and interrogation not only that Zephyr was the Princess of Crystotopia, but that she and her party were trying to find the Sword of Wonders.

"Don't you even try it!" Liz said loudly. "Aeria is one of the allied kingdoms! Once your associates find out that this is the Princess and her party, they'll lock you up and throw away the key!"

"You don't know do you girl?" Captain White Beard said. "The Dark Forces are beginning to thrive over all of Danus. Do you really think that our associates care anything about the allied kingdoms?! Aerian supporters of slavery aren't your most law-abiding citizens! They would love to get their hands on the daughter of a king, and they would just as easily turn you over to Scorpius himself!"

"Now," Captain White Beard said as he clapped his hands and faced his crew. "What lovely items have the Princess and her party brought for us eh?"

Chuckling, the pirate captain started holding up Zephyr and her friends' belongings as he named them.

"Some sacks of lucans," he said as he removed a silver and golden lucan from Zephyr's money supply and bit down on them. "We'll keep the money for ourselves."

"We have a few magic crystal spears, a magic crystal bow and quiver of arrows, and the armor of a Ruby Knight as well as his sword. That's sure to fetch a nice profit. We don't have much use for these ordinary spears that these white centaurs were carrying, but the centaurs and these black horses are a nice catch. You have some soggy and wet food in these satchels. But, it is still better than our own slop and well-cooked I might say. Then, some maps. They're a little wet, but we might be able to salvage them for a sale."

"And finally," Captain White Beard said as he eyed Zephyr. "There's what you were carrying Princess. Anything belonging to you is worth a treasury of lucans I'm sure."

Zephyr snorted as the pirate captain started to examine her own items.

"Some sort of bracelet," he said as he held up Zephyr's golden friendship bracelet. "We've got a crystal ring, a silver locket, and best of all, this...." Captain White Beard paused as he held up Wind Chaser, Zephyr's weapon.

"I wouldn't touch that if I were you!" Zephyr said angrily. "You can't have it! It belonged to my mother! It's one of the few things I have left to remember her by!"

"It's mine now," Captain White Beard said with a grimace. "I would sell it, but a weapon like this is too precious to part with."

Staring at Zephyr's weapon, Captain White Beard spit on it as he wiped it with his hand.

"I'll get you for this!" Zephyr said with gritted teeth.

But Captain White Beard walked away as he attached Zephyr's weapon to his belt.

"Can't you cast a spell or something?" Trinda asked Zephyr.

"Don't even try it!" one of the pirates said. "Those bonds are magic proof!"

Peering down, Zephyr saw that the ropes that held her and her friends were gray glowing bonds, and she recalled similar ones that had been used on her when she was held prisoner at Prince Wart's castle.

"Relax," one of the pirates said. "We'll be in Aeria shortly."

Then, the pirate crew left Zephyr and her party as they went about their business and hummed tunes to each other and sang pirate songs.

"I'm sorry, Your Highness," Peantos said sadly. "I've failed you."

"No, Peantos," Zephyr said. "You've been wonderful. You can't blame yourself for this."

"Okay," Liz said as she sighed and entered deep thought. "There's a solution to every problem. We just have to think."

"I don't think any amount of thinking can help us now," Trion said.

"Mmm," Liz whispered as something crossed her mind.

"Maybe it can," she said as she eyed Captain White Beard. "Maybe it can."

"Excuse me?" Zephyr said.

"If you concentrate, Zephyr," Liz whispered. "Perhaps you can get through to Wind Chaser and control it."

"No," Zephyr said as she shook her head. "I can't use magic, remember?"

"I know," Liz said. "Not directly. But the connection between you and that weapon isn't a type of direct magic. The magic is in the weapon, and it's more like a spiritual connection. It's magic yes, but it might not have anything to do with these bonds."

"I don't think it will work," Zephyr said quietly.

"I've seen you use the weapon, Zephyr," Brandon said. "Even though you usually have it in your hands first, it kind of seems like you use your mind to control it."

"Just try," Liz said. "Concentrate on Wind Chaser and these ropes. It's worth an attempt."

"Fine," Zephyr said with a sigh. "But, don't blame me if nothing happens."

Closing her eyes, Zephyr focused on the gray glowing bonds that held her party as well as Wind Chaser.

"It's working," Trinda whispered.

She noticed that the ancient markings on Zephyr's weapon were beginning to glow white.

Then, Wind Chaser shook a little, but it soon stopped glowing and moving at the same time, and Zephyr opened her eyes and took deep breaths.

"I told you it wouldn't work," she said.

"That's because you didn't believe it would," Liz said. "Try again, and this time, have faith that it will work."

"Alright," Zephyr said as she closed her eyes once more.

"It's going to work," she whispered to herself. "I have to believe."

Suddenly, Wind Chaser began to glow, and it took off from Captain White Beard's belt as it sped toward Cara's head.

"Duck!" Trion yelled, and Cara and the rest of Zephyr's party put their heads down.

In an instant, the ropes that held Zephyr and her friends were cut and broken, and Zephyr caught her weapon in the air.

"Quickly men!" Captain White Beard screamed. "They're escaping! We have to stop them!"

Though the pirates attacked Zephyr and her friends, they fought back. It was difficult for them to fight the pirates, for the attackers were armed, and out of all of Zephyr and her friends, only Zephyr had a weapon.

Fortunately, however, the pirates didn't want to hurt anyone. They were far too interested in the profit they would make from selling their captives into slavery.

But slowly, Zephyr's party was encircled and forced together as the pirates attempted to recapture them.

As a last desperate effort to escape, Zephyr closed her eyes and thought of Wind Chaser and the pirates, and her focus was more on the nearby locations of the pirates than on them directly—something which Zephyr had never before attempted.

Then, opening her eyes, Zephyr threw her weapon, and powerful winds swept Captain White Beard and his crew around and off of the ship.

Almost the entire pirate crew was knocked into the sea below, and the white centaurs and the fairy guards managed to force the others over the sides of the ship.

Yet, as Captain White Beard fell, he managed to take his sword and stick it into the right wing of the ship, and he held onto the sword to keep himself from falling.

"Curse the lot of you!" he yelled. "Captain White Beard will have his revenge!"

"Goodbye, Captain," Zephyr said.

Closing her eyes, she concentrated on Wind Chaser and Captain White Beard's location. Then, throwing her weapon, Zephyr produced gusts of wind that pushed the captain into the sky.

But, as Captain White Beard was tossed into the air, due to his grip on his sword, the ship's right wing was torn in half. Then, the pirate captain laughed as he and his sword plummeted into the sea along with half of the ship's right wing.

Just as Zephyr caught Wind Chaser, the ship began to descend rapidly as it continued to move forward.

Next, it began to fall at an angle, but the magic of the ship's remaining left wing made the ship go down at a somewhat steady pace.

"Brace yourselves!" Valon yelled.

"We're gonna die!" Tarn told Zephyr fearfully as she was thrown about.

It was really quite difficult for the horses and the white centaurs to keep their balance.

Helga fainted, and the rest of Zephyr's party grabbed onto the sides of the ship. Zephyr expected to hear a giant splash from the ship falling into the sea, but it was much more like a crash, and everyone was thrown in different directions as the pirate ship landed.

Then, peering overboard, everyone marveled as he observed the semblance of a beach.

"We're on land!" Thantos said with awe.

"Yes," Piro said. "But, it won't take long for those pirates to catch up to us, I'm sure. Even, if they do have to swim here."

"Where are we?" Trinda asked.

"Yeah," Liz said. "I thought we were headed for Aeria. We've got to be somewhere close to it."

"I should check to see if it's safe to go on," Sir Gallan said.

"Let us go," Reen said as he eyed Thantos and Peantos. "We can fly in the air and move quicker than you Sir Gallan."

"Is anyone hurt?" Little Herb asked.

"I'm hurt!" Tarn said to Little Herb. *"I think I got a splinter in my leg from that boat!"*

Unfortunately, Little Herb could not talk to animals, but Zephyr heard what Tarn said.

"It's alright," she told the horse as she patted her mane. *"You're in good hands."*

"Little Herb," Zephyr called. "I think my horse needs medical attention. Could you look at her?"

"Certainly," Little Herb responded, and he ran over to Tarn quickly.

Thantos, Peantos, and Reen recovered their crystal spears from the ship and took off to survey the land.

"You know," Sir Gallan said as he put his hand on Brandon's shoulder. "You were very brave to come after me and to face King Seadon. And, you fought well...for a boy of course."

"Thanks," Brandon said. "I think...anyway."

"Maybe...maybe there's a chance that you will become a knight someday."

"What?" Brandon said with wide eyes.

"Well uh...maybe," Sir Gallan said reluctantly. "It still remains to be seen." Brandon beamed at Sir Gallan, but the Ruby Knight cleared his throat and walked away.

"At least we got everything back that they took from us," Trinda said. "It's all still on the ship."

Slowly, Zephyr's party scoured the pirate ship as they salvaged the items that had been taken from them.

"We're lucky to be alive," Brandon said as he recovered his crystal sword. "To just think that I almost married a whale."

"Yes," Zephyr said as she laughed and put on her crystal ring, locket, and friendship bracelet. "That would have been a disaster!"

"I'm more concerned about my physical condition and the fact that I haven't had a full night's sleep," Trinda said with a sigh.

"We can't stop now," Liz said. "Those pirates are close by I'm sure."

"So!" Trinda said in a loud voice. "Everything has to be so logical to you doesn't it, Liz?! Well, I think it's logical to reason that I'm tired, I'm hungry, and I've nearly been sold into slavery! So, I think a break is in order!"

"Calm down!" Brandon said. "I'm sure we can take a minute to eat something." Digging into a recovered satchel, he removed a few soggy sandwiches and gave one to Trinda, Liz, and Zephyr.

"That's a good idea," Zephyr said with a smile. "There's always time to eat."

Reaching into a satchel, she took out another sandwich and held it under an unconscious Helga's nose.

Then, the dwarf bolted up hastily.

"I smell Gusto's food!" she said excitedly. "I can identify the scent of his cooking from a mile away! No one cooks like him!"

"It's just a soggy sandwich," Zephyr said with a smirk.

But Helga took the sandwich from Zephyr and bit into it as her sapphire eyes sparkled.

"Oh, Gusto," she said. "I can almost taste you."

"Really, Helga?" Zephyr said. "You will see him again. Don't worry."

"Maybe we should worry," Liz said.

"What are you talking about Liz?" Brandon asked.

"There's no telling what is going on in Crystotopia right now," she said. "We can only hope that all is well."

"Well, can't Zephyr see what's happening with magic," Trinda said. "I mean through Scorn."

"Yeah," Zephyr said as she sat down with a blank stare on her face. "But, I don't know if I want to see it. I fear the worst."

"Oh, you're probably right, Your Highness," Helga said as she hugged her tightly. "Everything we love might be gone."

Tears streamed rapidly down the nursemaid's face.

"Get yourselves together!" Trinda said. "You have to be strong, and there's only one way to tell what's really going on. The truth isn't always pretty, like me, but it's certainly worth knowing."

"You're right," Zephyr said as she stood abruptly, and Helga lost her balance and fell backward. "I have to stay strong. Why, I'm a diplomatic official."

"Here it goes," she said as she rubbed her crystal ring.

Then, she gulped and closed her eyes as she took her spell-casting position. Through her thoughts, she flashed the words, "Sightus Impetus Executo!" and whirled her fingers, causing images to appear in her head.

She could see trees and green grass and what looked like millions of tiny dots below her that were blurred together and moving like atoms.

"Scorn," Zephyr thought. *"Scorn, can you hear me?"*

"Yes, Zephyr," Scorn replied through his mind. *"I can hear you."*

"How's it going? Is everyone safe?"

"I'm afraid not, Zephyr. The battle has started, and the Dark Forces are attacking Crystotopia. The armies of the allied kingdoms are fighting along with your father, but the Dark Forces have a new weapon."

"A weapon!" Zephyr thought with surprise. *"What is it?"*

"I'll show you."

Soaring through the sky, Scorn began to descend. He dodged several arrows that were launched into the air, and as he approached the ground, Zephyr saw something that made her feel as though her heart were shattering.

Giant and magnificent flames engulfed the ground below and were overpowering hordes of fairy guards and white centaurs. And, in the center of the flames and floating in the sky with skin the color of sand, cinnamon eyes that were burning red with fire, and flaming red hair, was Cor.

Only, Cor wasn't helping the allied kingdoms, but he was attacking them with the power of the Great Flame of Ember. And, the allied kingdoms' armies seemed as though they could barely withstand the strength and magnitude of his magic.

But, Zephyr could also see that with blue eyes, oak-colored hair, and golden brown skin Queen Astra of Glacionus was fighting Cor directly with her magic necklace of ice.

It seemed, however, that she was struggling to hold him off with her powers, and Cor's flames were spreading everywhere.

Also, Zephyr realized that the Dark Forces had the allied kingdoms' armies surrounded and were driving them back toward Quartz City and the Crystal Castle. Suddenly, Scorn flew higher as he avoided more arrows.

"No, Scorn!" Zephyr thought with despair. *"Why is Cor working with the Dark Forces?!"*

"Syphron thinks that King Scorpius put a curse on him. But, no one has been able to break it, let alone get close enough to Cor to try. Your father thinks he could break the curse if he had the Sword of Wonders but...."

"Can they stop Cor somehow without hurting him?"

"I don't know. But right now, Cor is oppressing the allied kingdoms' armies. The Great Flame of Ember is tremendously potent. And, the other threat is King Vigor and his Emerald Knights. At least, we don't have to deal with King Seadon and his trident. The water wizard, General Bubble Toe is leading Vainaquia's forces. And, King Scorpius isn't fighting either. We think that's a good thing, but Syphron suspects that he's up to something."

"Scorn, tell Syphron to try and stall and keep Cor alive. I'll get to the Sword of Wonders as soon as I can."

"They're trying not to hurt him, but he's doing us more harm than we are him. Have you gotten to Aeria and the Oracles yet?"

"We'll be there shortly. Don't be concerned about me Scorn. Take care of yourself."

"Very well. Goodbye, Zephyr."

Opening her eyes, Zephyr broke the enchantment between her and Scorn.

"Well," Liz said. "How bad is it?"

"It's bad," Zephyr said as she shook her head. "It's very bad. For starters, Cor is under a curse, and he's doing a number on the allied kingdoms' armies with the Great Flame of Ember."

"No!" Helga said with a shriek. "He can't!"

"We have to stop him somehow without harming him," Zephyr said. "The sooner we get to the Sword of Wonders, the better. Cor is doing a lot of damage, you guys."

"Yes, Your Highness," Helga said. "We have to hurry. Where are those fairy guards?!"

Just as Helga spoke, Peantos and Reen landed in front of Zephyr.

"Your Highness," Peantos said. "We have scouted the area, and we've come across the Great Stair, which should lead us to Aeria. It is heavily guarded by air wizards, but Reen and I have informed the guards of your intentions and business in the air kingdom. They have granted us safe passage onto the Great Stair and into Aeria."

"Thank you," Zephyr said. "But, where is Thantos?"

"I don't know," Reen said. "He was right behind us the last I checked."

"Here I am, Your Highness!" Thantos said as he landed suddenly. "I was just doing some extra surveying of the area."

"Good," Sir Gallan said. "Now that we are all accounted for, we can push forward."

"Wait!" Trion said as he eyed Thantos. "Fairy guard, where is your crystal spear?"

"Oh," Thantos said. "I'm afraid I dropped it because I was moving so hastily. But, it can't be helped now."

"That's alright!" Sir Gallan said with a laugh. "We all have plenty of weapons to go around. So, the rest of us will protect you. Come on!"

Gathering their belongings, Zephyr and her party set off as they headed towards the Great Stair.

Aeria, as Zephyr had heard, was a kingdom in the sky made entirely of cloud, but the land below the kingdom possessed nothing but barren and solid rock.

So, traveling to the Great Stair was anything but easy, and Tarn complained of aches and pains from the rough and rocky terrain constantly.

But then, before anyone knew it, the party came upon what Zephyr thought was the tallest mountain she had ever seen.

However, as the party drew closer to it, Zephyr realized that a twisting staircase made of rock had been formed in the mountain and wrapped its way around it, and reached up into the sky.

"The Great Stair," Helga whispered. "It sure doesn't look dwarf-friendly."

When Zephyr and her party finally reached the edge of the Great Stair, they encountered a band of men with white hair and white eyes who were dressed in white and gray armor, and Zephyr knew that they were air wizards and guards.

"Where is the Princess?" one of them asked, and Zephyr's friends pointed to her.

Then, the air wizard approached Zephyr and bowed as he kissed her hand.

"Your Highness," he said with a smile. "We are glad you made it here safely."

"Thank you, air wizard," Zephyr said. "So, this is the famed Great Stair. It looks.. .challenging."

"Ha!" the air wizard said with a laugh. "Yes, it is a bit much. We would use our magic to fly you to Aeria. However, Aeria's council has forbidden us to use our magic to do such things. We are in wartime, and the council wants to monitor everyone who enters and leaves the kingdom carefully. So, we may only use the Great Stair to reach Aeria."

"But this is an emergency," Sir Gallan said. "We need to see the Oracles immediately!"

"I'm sorry," the guard said. "Orders are orders. I couldn't help you if I tried. There are now spells in place to keep people from using magic to reach the kingdom anyway."

"But, we were on a pirate ship that was going to Aeria by way of magic," Cara said. "The pirates seemed unaware of such defensive measures."

"They couldn't have known," the guard said. "These measures have just been put into place ever since the attack on Crystotopia started a couple of days ago."

"But...." Liz started to say.

However, Zephyr cut her off.

"Come on," she said with a sigh. "We can't keep arguing. Let's get started. It seems like quite a hike."

So, Zephyr and her party reluctantly began the long climb up the Great Stair. It also was no simple task, for the staircase was rough, and each step was excessively large, making it a difficult journey for the white centaurs and the horses.

As Trinda climbed the staircase, she counted each step, but she lost count after a hundred. Eventually, Helga was completely out of breath and had to be carried under Trion's arm. Even the fairy guards were weary and were barely able to flap their wings.

"Let's...turn back!" Helga said as she panted. "This is way too high and far!"

"Whatever you do, don't look down!" Sir Gallan said.

"This is making my stomach very queasy!" Tarn said. *"I can't go on, Zephyr!"*

"Just stay focused," Zephyr told the horse. *"I'm sure we're almost there."*

Then suddenly, Valon's foot slipped, and he fell to the side.

However, Peantos grabbed his arm quickly and flapped his wings furiously as he struggled to help him to his feet.

"I never thought I would see the day when my life would be saved by a fairy," Valon said with a smile.

"I never thought I would either," Peantos said.

He pulled as hard as he could, but Valon was still slipping and slowly falling. But Reen grabbed Peantos' waist and helped him pull both himself and Valon to safety. Then, Valon continued to climb the Great Stair, and Peantos and Reen landed behind him as they followed him.

"Keep going," Sir Gallan said. "Not much farther now!"

"Why did they make these stairs so big and difficult to climb?" Trinda asked.

"It is rumored that the Great Stair was created by giants," Helga said. "But, it's only a rumor."

"It makes sense when you think about the size of these steps!" Brandon said. "They're huge!"

Soon, Zephyr and her party were dirty, exhausted, and pushed to the limit.

And, after what seemed like an eternity of traversing the Great Stair, the party seemed as if it could go on no longer.

Each movement Zephyr and her friends made was slow, and the growing altitude and cold windy atmosphere seemed impossible to deal with nor adaptable.

"No...no more," Zephyr said.

"Just a little further," Sir Gallan said as he took a deep breath.

However, as he put his hand on the next step, he fell off of his horse and landed on the step below him.

Then, the rest of the party, seeing Sir Gallan fall and collapse, lost hope and will as they collapsed as well. And, all seemed lost.

Chapter 9

The Oracles of Aeria

Zephyr sat up to find herself on the most comfortable bed she had ever been on. But surprisingly, the bed was made of thick and fluffy white clouds. Yet, compared to the old mattress that Zephyr used to sleep on in the Krumple's home on Earth, she felt this was one hundred and fifty percent better.

As Zephyr observed her surroundings, she realized that clouds and cloud objects were all around her—clouds that she could walk on and touch.

Then, a door of cloud opened, and an air witch with neatly braided white hair, tan skin, and white eyes entered. She was dressed in a maid's uniform, and she was carrying a tray on which rested biscuits and a white bubbling liquid in a glass.

"You're awake," she said in a cheerful voice as she sat the tray she held on a table beside Zephyr. "Master Air Walker predicted you would wake up today. You and your friends have been asleep for a day and a half. The guards at the entrance to Galeon found you in quite a state, and you poor things almost died from exerting yourselves too much."

"Oh," Zephyr said as she held her head. "Is that what happened? Everything seems like a daze or a dream."

Feeling her stomach rumble with hunger, she helped herself to the biscuits the maid had sat on the table by her bed.

"This is delicious!" she said with her mouth full.

"Fluffy Cloud Biscuits," the maid said with a grin.

Then, Zephyr drank some of the white bubbling liquid and smiled.

"What is this?" she asked as she held up the glass.

"It's Wind Whipped Nimbus Juice," the maid answered. "Tastes like a breath of fresh air."

"Yes," Zephyr said. "It most certainly does."

"Where am I?" she asked as she glanced around the room once more.

"You're in Master Air Walker's home in the City of Galeon, the capital of Aeria. Master Air Walker had you and your friends brought here to recuperate."

"Who is he?" Zephyr asked as she wrinkled her brow.

"Why, he's the President of Aeria's Governing Council of course."

"Believe me, Princess," the maid said with a laugh. "You're safe."

"Where are my friends? Are they in separate rooms?"

"Most of them are awake already. They should be relaxing downstairs. Master Air Walker asked me to tell you to feel free to explore his home, and he will be here shortly."

"Thank you," Zephyr said. "And, who are you?"

"I'm Rainera," the maid said as she curtsied. "Master Air Walker's servant. You may call me if you need anything."

Then slowly, Rainera left the room.

As Zephyr stood and jumped off of the bed, she observed her clothing and saw that she had been dressed in a plain white nightgown and slippers.

Moving next to the bed, she removed a soft white robe that was hanging beside her and put it on.

As she walked over to the door, Zephyr felt funny about touching a doorknob made of a cloud.

But as she gripped the doorknob and opened the door, she found that it seemed like any other. As Zephyr went outside the room, she gasped as she surveyed Master Air Walker's home.

Apparently, it was quite large. Zephyr had to walk down a long corridor and pass at least seven rooms as well as many pieces of furniture including desks, chairs, and tables, before she came to anything that looked like a staircase.

Then, as she descended the staircase, she found Helga, Peantos, Sir Gallan, Thantos, Reen, and Elizabeth resting in chairs and on sofas on the lower level. They were all crowded around a cloud fireplace, which seemed to be emitting warm but windy air.

"Zephyr!" Liz called. "You're awake!"

"Yes," Zephyr said happily. "But, I didn't expect to end up here."

"Well it's a lot better than ending up in slavery," Helga said.

"I suppose," Zephyr said as she looked around. "Where are the others?"

"Trinda, Brandon, and Little Herb haven't woken up yet," Helga said. "They're in guest rooms upstairs, and the white centaurs and the horses are in Master Air Walker's stable outside."

"A serious mistake on Master Air Walker's part," Peantos said as he shook his head. "To put the centaurs in the stable."

"Oh, and why is that?" Zephyr asked.

"All centaurs hate being compared to horses. We saw Cara, Valon, Piro, and Trion earlier, and they were complaining because they were put in the stable and given horse feed. They feel they should have been given room and board in Master Air Walker's home."

"I hope they aren't terribly offended," Zephyr said.

"They should be grateful that they are alive," Thantos said. "Master Air Walker is very kind to allow us to even stay in his home and help us recover. Centaurs are so ignorant."

"No," Liz said. "They probably don't really mean it."

"I'm anxious to meet this Master Air Walker," Zephyr said. "I wonder where he is."

"Right on time I hope," someone said in a deep voice.

Everyone turned to see a heavyset bald man with dark chocolate skin and white eyes. He was dressed in fancy black and white clothing, and as he approached Zephyr, he bowed.

"It is an honor to make your acquaintance, Your Highness," he said as he kissed Zephyr's hand.

"Thank you, Master Air Walker," Zephyr said. "We are in your debt."

"Oh don't worry about that," Master Air Walker said with a laugh. "And you may call me Cloud."

"Well...Cloud," Zephyr said. "We have come to Aeria to seek the advice of the Oracles, and we don't have a moment to lose. We've probably been set back already from all the sleeping we've done. My friends and I are on a quest to find the Sword of Wonders, and as we speak, the Dark Forces are attacking Crystotopia. Without the sword, my father may never win the battle."

"Oh yes, I see," Cloud said. "The word of the sword's disappearance has spread like wildfire. But, I am surprised that King Lionus has only just now sought the Oracles' advice."

"No," Sir Gallan said as he shook his head. "The King sent a party weeks ago to seek their advice, but it never came back."

"This is terrible!" Cloud said as he sighed and lowered his head. "Foul play on the Dark Forces' part! I'm sure of it!"

"Please," Zephyr said. "Take us to the Oracles, and we will be on our way."

"I will do more than that, Your Highness," Master Air Walker said. "I've noticed that your rations are dwindling and your food has become extremely...soggy. I will provide your party with enough food to last you for several weeks, and I will guarantee you safe and swift passage out of Aeria. Also, I will arrange a trip to Aeria's finest spa here in Galeon. It is called Airlution. You and your party were in such bad condition, and some pampering might do you some good."

"You are very kind," Zephyr said. "And, I will accept all that you offer except for the trip to the spa. It is a detour to my party and I cannot afford it."

"No!" someone yelled from behind Zephyr.

Zephyr turned to see Trinda Temple descending the staircase with her eyes wide open. "You can't possibly turn down a trip to the spa, Zephyr! Are you mad?!"

"Trinda," Zephyr said. "We've got to stick to our agenda."

"May we go to see the Oracles?" Zephyr asked Master Air Walker as she faced him.

"They are extremely busy," he replied. "However, I'm sure they would put aside a moment to see you."

"Great!" Zephyr said happily. "We'll get ready."

"I'm afraid there is no 'we,'" Cloud said. "The Oracles only see one person at a once. So, you must go to them alone. I've had Rainera wash and dry your clothing, and it should be in your room with your belongings. As soon as you are prepared, I will take you to the Oracles' temple."

"Well," Trinda said. "Zephyr might not want to go to the spa, but I'm all for it. We can go there while she sticks to her 'agenda.'"

"No, Trinda!" Zephyr said angrily. "No spa!"

"What else are we going to do while we wait for you to come back? We'll just be sitting around."

"Oh, you're impossible, Trinda," Zephyr said as she shook her head. "Fine. You may go to the spa. But, the minute I return from the Oracles, we are leaving."

"Good!" Cloud said as he clapped his hands. "I'll set everything up, and I'll be back soon."

Then, he hurried out of the house.

Zephyr and her friends got themselves dressed and ready to leave. Zephyr was to go see the Oracles and the rest of her party was to go to Galeon's spa, Airlution.

Master Air Walker escorted Zephyr to the Oracles himself along with guards for their protection.

And, it was a most interesting experience to go through any part of Aeria. The cloud kingdom was engulfed and encircled by heavy winds, thunder, lightning, snow, and sleet, as well as lots of sun in various places.

But the citizens of Aeria hardly seemed to notice the natural wonders and disturbances around them.

And, as Zephyr walked through the streets of Galeon, she saw many strange things. Random air wizards and witches kept trying to offer to tell her future. Vehicles made of clouds flew about in the air, transporting people to and fro. And, there were many foods for sale that tasted fresh and pure and that were produced with different types of wind or clouds.

But what was really most fascinating to Zephyr was the Oracles' temple. It was made out of white, black, and gray cloud parts as well as white and black marble. Surrounding the temple were lightning rods, which after each second were all struck by lightning simultaneously. Also, a long line of people stretched from the outside to inside of the temple, all of them waiting to seek the Oracles' advice and guidance.

However, the people stepped aside as soon as they saw Master Air Walker and Zephyr approaching the temple.

"Coming through," the guards said. "Make way for Master Air Walker!"

As Master Air Walker led Zephyr inside the temple, she gasped with disbelief, for the entire ceiling inside was lined with stars. Also, there was a long narrow path leading to a pair of large white doors in the distance. On opposite sides of the path, there were streams of flowing water, in which rain fell at a constant rate.

Master Air Walker took Zephyr to the pair of double white doors at the end of the path where a guard stood dressed in white and gray armor.

"Master Air Walker," he said as he cleared his throat. "What brings you to the temple?"

"I'm on important business," Master Air Walker replied. "Tell the Oracles that the Princess of Crystotopia has come to see them."

"Of course, sir," the guard said as he gave a salute.

Then, he opened one of the white doors and slipped inside. Zephyr tried to see what lay behind the open door, but the guard closed it hastily.

But, after a minute, he came back and opened both doors.

"The Oracles will see you now," he told Zephyr. "Apparently, they have been expecting you."

Zephyr looked at Master Air Walker nervously and with hesitation.

"Go ahead," he told her. "You have nothing to fear."

Then, taking a deep breath, Zephyr walked into the room.

It was so bright inside that she could barely see a thing. But after a second, her eyes adjusted, and she could see clearly.

Zephyr was inside a humongous room supported by white, gray, and black marble pillars as well as a clear floor and ceiling of glass. Ahead of her sat three golden thrones that were arranged in such a fashion that they resembled a triangle.

And, on the thrones, there were three figures, who couldn't be seen due to the fact that they were covered by cloaks and unusual masks. Also, there were small clouds hovering above their heads, and each one matched the color of the masks the people below the clouds were wearing.

There was a white cloud, below which sat a person wearing a white mask on the first throne to the left. Next, there was a gray cloud, below which sat a person wearing a gray mask positioned on the throne in the center of the other two. And finally, there was a black cloud hovering above a person with a black mask who sat on the last throne to the right of the other two. Remaining completely still, Zephyr examined the three strangers in front of her.

"Come forward, Princess," all three voices said together.

Even though each of the three people on the thrones was speaking, it seemed like they were saying the same things simultaneously in unison. Also, Zephyr was sure it sounded much more like one person talking in an eerie high-pitched voice.

"Come forward," the Oracles said again.

Moving closer to the three thrones and figures before her, Zephyr spoke.

"I...I have come to seek your advice Great Oracles," she said with a stutter. "I need to know the whereabouts of the Sword of Wonders."

"We know why you have come," the Oracles said. "But you must know, what you seek shall not be easy to obtain."

95

"Yes," Zephyr said. "But I have to do it. My father needs the sword to be retrieved and brought back to Crystotopia."

"What you seek no longer belongs to your father."

"What?" Zephyr said as she shook her head with confusion. "I don't understand."

"At the turn of each new century, the Sword of Wonders returns to the place of its birth. There it will stay until it is claimed by its new owner."

"New owner?" Zephyr repeated with a frown.

"A century ago, the royal family of Crystotopia claimed the Sword of Wonders, and it passed through their bloodline for a hundred years. Now, the sword will lend its power to the bloodline of whoever claims it this century."

"But where is the sword?" Zephyr asked.

"Only one creature can lead you to the Sword of Wonders. This creature has been there since the dawn of time and the birth of the sword. It is the sword's true guardian."

"What creature is this?"

"It is the most magical, beautiful, and mystical of beings. Only the pure of heart can find the creature, and only the brave may follow its path."

"But what is it exactly?"

"When the trees whisper, when the clouds race, and when the second moon of Danus and the sun are one, only then shall the creature reveal itself."

"That doesn't make any sense," Zephyr said.

However, the Oracles didn't say anything else, so Zephyr turned around and started to leave feeling disappointed.

"One more thing Princess," the Oracles said, and Zephyr stopped moving as she listened.

"We know that you wish to use the sword to save the heir to Ember. But only after you reach the sword's birthplace will you realize the Ancient Magic needed to break the curse on him. It is also the key needed to recover the sword, for the sword is also naturally governed by this magic. That is why just before its disappearance, the sword lent its power to you to fulfill your earthling wish for you to attend your junior prom with Ember's heir. And that is why it restored your human friends' memories and had them brought back to Danus. For just before the turn of the new century, the Sword of Wonders though still tied to you, realized that you possessed the Ancient Magic inside of you as well as the potential to claim the sword for your bloodline during the next century, and events were set in motion to give you the opportunity to realize this magic and wield the true power of the sword—events that involve your friends and those for who you possess concern. But, if you succeed remains to be seen, and is a task of which only you can decide the outcome."

"Thank you," Zephyr said.

She gasped and sighed sadly, for she had no idea what the Oracles meant by everything they had told her. Yet, she was determined to figure it out as she scurried away to regroup with her friends and continue with her journey.

Chapter 10

The Silver Unicorn

When Zephyr got to Airlution, Trinda was busy trying to experience all of the spa's services, including the Air Lift, and the Wind Massage. Liz and Zephyr had to drag Trinda out of the spa to get her to leave.

"No!" Trinda yelled as Zephyr and Liz forced her out of the front door. "I just need another minute! I haven't finished my Breeze Facial!"

"Get a grip, Trinda," Liz said. "It's time to go."

"You don't understand!" Trinda screamed. "I need this!"

Once Zephyr and her friends were outside, Master Air Walker arranged transportation to escort the party out of Aeria. However, travel back through Vainaquia was far too dangerous. So, Zephyr and her party were instead heading north to the kingdom of Silveron. Once there, they could journey east to Sandus and return to Crystotopia by going south across the desert kingdom.

Zephyr explained to her party exactly what the Oracles had told her, particularly the riddle about the creature that could lead her to the Sword of Wonders. But, no one understood the meaning of the Oracles' words.

"When the trees whisper, when the clouds race, and when the second moon of Danus and the sun are one, only then shall the creature reveal itself," Liz said as she looked into the sky around her. "That's quite a conundrum."

She and the rest of the party were flying on a giant cloud car to the edge of Silveron along with several Aerian guards.

"Speak in English brainiac!" Trinda said.

"I mean, it's a difficult puzzle," Liz said. "I know I can figure it out. It's probably right under our noses."

"Right now, I'm concerned about this cloud car," Piro said. "I'm a centaur, and I'm not supposed to be flying."

"Flying is the only way to travel," Peantos said with a laugh as he flapped his wings.

"We're just so far away from the ground," Helga said. "I can't wait till I'm back on the dirt and standing on my own two feet."

"I'm just glad that Master Air Walker gave us some new maps," Little Herb said. "I couldn't make out the old ones anymore."

"Stop talking and focus on the words of the Oracles," Zephyr said. "We have to figure this out."

"I'm surprised the Oracles told you all of that," Sir Gallan said. "They usually hardly say anything and barely even give a hint. They must have liked you."

"What?" Zephyr said with shock.

"Oh, not to mean that anyone wouldn't like you, Your Highness," Sir Gallan said as he waved his hands at Zephyr. "Of course, they liked you. Anyone would."

"Really," Liz said with a laugh. "That's a Freudian slip if I ever heard one."

"We're approaching Silveron, Your Highness," one of the Aerian guards that were guiding the cloud car said.

Peering down, Zephyr observed that in place of the barren and rocky terrain beneath Aeria, there were rich green trees and grass.

Then, the cloud car transport descended slowly, and soon it landed on the ground with ease.

"Well you're quite the busy one aren't you?" Tarn said to Zephyr once she got out of the cloud car safely. *"I haven't seen such excitement since my birth. You know, it's not every day that a horse gets turned into a sea creature or flies through the sky. I'm just in awe that I'm still alive, especially with my fear of heights."*

"I apologize Tarn," Zephyr said as she rubbed the horse's mane. *"I wish it weren't so difficult. I hope it gets better."*

"Are you kidding? Being with you is a lot more interesting than being cooped up in some stable. You only live once."

"Thanks," Zephyr said.

"This is as far as we can take you, Your Highness," one of the Aerian guards said. "May the Oracles foretell of your success."

"Thank you," Zephyr said. "Please give Master Air Walker my regards."

Then, Zephyr and her party mounted their horses and the white centaurs as they started traveling through Silveron and following Little Herb's directions.

The edge of Silveron was somewhat similar to the Great Stair of Aeria. Both were surrounded by guards who questioned Zephyr and her friends' motives.

Surprisingly, however, the guards in Silveron didn't trust that Zephyr was the Princess of Crystotopia or anything she said, but they were more accepting and sure of Sir Gallan's words because they could tell that he was a Ruby Knight.

Once Zephyr and her friends made it by several guard checkpoints, they managed to journey for a day through Silveron, and they stopped in Silver City, for a quick rest.

Amazingly, living up to its name, Silver City possessed buildings and houses made of silver, and the people seemed quite wealthy and sophisticated. Why even the streets were paved in silver?

Trinda begged to stay in the city and do some shopping as she spotted numerous fancy and luxurious clothes and expensive silver trinkets for sale, but Zephyr was much too concerned that everyone move as quickly as he could to reach Crystotopia to check on her father and seek help to decipher the words of the Oracles.

Plus, the Silverians' extravagant silver jewelry, fine clothing, and self-absorbed and superficial personalities kept reminding Zephyr of the unpleasant and rude people in Vainaquia, who cared only about themselves. And, the people in Silver City seemed just as selfish and self-centered, which made Zephyr very uncomfortable.

But even as night began to approach, Zephyr still wanted to keep moving. Yet, the entire party expressed their feelings of wanting to rest.

So, finally, when Zephyr could no longer see in the dark, she agreed that she and her friends should stop for the night. And everyone settled down as soon as he reached a wood next to a flowing stream of clear blue water.

"We should stay alert," Trion said.

"Why?" Zephyr asked. "Silveron is one of the allied kingdoms. We have nothing to fear here."

"You heard what those pirates said," Brandon told her. "The Dark Forces are all over Danus."

"He's right, Your Highness," Helga said. "And don't forget that Madam Vitaria is from this kingdom."

"Oh yeah!" Zephyr said as her eyes widened.

She recalled her stuck-up governess who turned out to be a spy and an agent for the Dark Forces.

"Perhaps we should seek the protection of King Trump," she said.

"If he's anything like Madam Vitaria, I don't think it's worth the trouble," Brandon said.

"Well, I've never met King Trump before," Zephyr said. "And, I don't know what he's like. Although, my father did say that he was vain."

"See, there you go!" Brandon said. "Vain! The people here are just like Seadon and his daughter! I can't wait to get out of this kingdom, and I don't care how nice and pretty it is!"

"We won't be able to meet King Trump anyway," Thantos said. "Every ruler of the allied kingdoms is fighting in Crystotopia against the Dark Forces."

"But Master Air Walker was in Aeria," Liz said. "Why wasn't he in battle?"

"Aeria is an exception," Thantos said. "It is ruled by a council, and although several council members are fighting in the battle with Aeria's army, Master Air Walker was left behind to take care of political matters in the kingdom."

"You certainly know a lot about the battle," Trion said as he wrinkled his brow.

"I serve and protect Crystotopia," Thantos said. "It is my job to know what is happening in the kingdom so that I may better carry out my duties."

"I don't trust you fairy," Trion said suspiciously as he narrowed his eyes. "I'm watching you!"

"Whatever!" Thantos said with a laugh.

Zephyr sat down and sighed sadly.

"I need some sort of sign or something," she said. "Some sort of clue to help me figure out the Oracles' words. Without discovering their meaning, we won't be able to find the Sword of Wonders, and we need to find it soon...before it's too late."

Taking a deep breath, Zephyr put her head in her hands.

"I should see how the battle is going," she said suddenly. "But, I can't bear knowing without being able to do anything. Now, I feel so helpless."

"Don't think about that now, Princess," Thantos said as he put his hand on her shoulder. "You should rest. I'm sure everything will be fine. The battle has only just begun."

"You're right," Zephyr said. "Thank you, Thantos."

Zephyr closed her eyes and lay down as she tried to rest by a group of weeping willows with thick overbearing green leaves. Although she was filled with worry about the people she loved and her helplessness to save them, she eventually drifted off to sleep.

***

"Is she the one? I thought she would be taller!"

"I'm sure she'll be fine. She is Andromeda's daughter after all."

"She may be her daughter, but she's certainly nothing like her. Why just by looking at Andromeda, you could tell she had strength. There's nothing strong about this one."

"Why doesn't she wake up? You may be right. She should have woken up by now."

"Well, she's still learning I suppose. I'll try and see if I can tickle her a little to help her on her way."

"Oh stop," Zephyr said as she felt something on her face. "Let me sleep just another minute, Helga."

Just then, as something tickled Zephyr's nose, she bolted up quickly.

"ACHOO!" she sneezed.

Zephyr peered about herself, and she saw that her entire party was asleep, even Valon, who was supposed to be on night watch.

"That's funny," she said to herself. "I could have sworn that I heard voices just now. And something was tickling my face."

"You're losing it," Zephyr whispered as she shook her head. "Keep it together."

Standing, she walked over to the nearby stream of water and bent over to get a drink.

But while Zephyr was drinking the water, a heavy wind blew through her hair, and she thought she heard voices again.

"Why isn't she saying anything? Is she deaf?"

"Who's there?" Zephyr asked as she turned around.

She immediately noticed that the wind was blowing through the trees, and it almost looked like the weeping willows she had been sleeping under were waving at her.

"Hello, there! Over here!"

Then, Zephyr was almost certain that the weeping willows in front of her were talking to her in a low voice, almost a whisper.

Moving forward, she approached them cautiously.

"Is that you?" she asked as she squinted. *"Are you trees talking to me?"*

"We most certainly are," one of the trees said. *"I knew you could hear us."*

"I...I knew I could talk to animals," Zephyr said with a stutter. *"But, I never knew I could talk to trees too."*

"Oh well of course you can't," one of the trees said softly. *"Well, what I mean is only on special occasions. Normally, we can't talk. But, I've waited my whole life since I was a young sapling for this moment, and we had to wake you to make sure that you didn't miss it."*

"Miss what?" Zephyr asked.

"You'll see," one of the trees told her. *"Your mother was the last person to have such a special honor. It makes perfect sense that you, her own young sapling, should be the next to experience it. And, a whole lifetime can go by without it happening. You've got to be chosen, and sometimes it takes a whole century before someone of that caliber is born or comes along."*

"I don't get it," Zephyr said.

"Shh!" the trees said. *"Quiet! It's time!"*

Zephyr had no idea what the trees were trying to tell her, and she looked about cluelessly as she waited for something to transpire. However, nothing did.

But just as she was about to kindly ask the weeping willows to let her get some sleep, Zephyr saw something amazing.

The darkened clouds in the sky began to move and pick up pace and move faster and faster until they raced through the air.

Then, the sun rose slowly, signifying that dawn was approaching. Yet, as the sun rose into the sky, the three moons of Danus still graced the world of magic with their light, and the second moon seemed to move mysteriously towards the sun until they were on top of each other, and the moon was blocking the sun completely.

"The words of Oracles," Zephyr said under her breath. "When the trees whisper, when the clouds race, and when the second moon of Danus and the sun are one, only then shall the creature reveal itself."

As the eclipse ended, and the sun and the second moon of Danus moved away from each other, the light from each struck the ground in front of Zephyr, and she saw a shadow dancing in the stream.

And slowly, the most beautiful creature Zephyr had ever seen appeared in front of her.

She was speechless and frightened as she gazed into the shining gray eyes of a sparkling silver unicorn—a creature with such breathtaking features that Zephyr sank to her knees and almost cried.

"You," Zephyr said. *"You! You're the creature, aren't you?! You're the guardian of the Sword of Wonders!"*

"Yes," the unicorn answered. *"I am the guardian of the sword, for I am the silver unicorn."*

"I can't believe this," Zephyr said. *"You're so beautiful! And, you knew my mother. The trees said so, and I remember Queen Astra telling the story of how my mother rode on a silver unicorn. Are you the same creature?"*

"There is and always has been only one silver unicorn. I was here when this world was new, and I shall be here when it is no more."

"Please, can you take me to the Sword of Wonders? My father is in battle, and he needs the sword to help him defeat the Dark Forces."

"I can take you to the sword," the unicorn said. *"If you are brave enough to follow. But, I cannot promise that you will live long enough to see the sword, or that you will be in time to save your father."*

"Couldn't you help us as a favor...a favor to my mother?"

"I do no favors. I only play my role in events, in which fate wishes me to participate."

"But..."

"Hurry!" the unicorn said. *"You must wake your friends immediately. We must leave, and if you wish to find the Sword of Wonders, you must follow me. Though, it may lead to your ruin."*

The silver unicorn walked a little further into the wood and stopped to wait for Zephyr.

As quickly as she could, Zephyr shook her party and told them to get ready.

"What's the rush?" Trinda asked. "Do you have a weak bladder?"

"It's the creature...the creature that the Oracles spoke of!" Zephyr explained hastily. "It's waiting for us to follow it!"

Zephyr pointed towards the silver unicorn, and her entire party gasped.

"Who's the newbie?" Tarn asked Zephyr. *"She looks so unnatural."*

"Yes. *It is quite a sight, Tarn,*" Zephyr responded. "*But she will lead us to what we've been searching for.*"

"It's like a ghost," Elizabeth said. "That unicorn is stunning! I've never seen anything like it!"

The entire party stopped to gaze at the silver unicorn's beauty, and Helga sobbed quietly.

"*I'm losing patience, Princess!*" the unicorn told Zephyr.

"*We're almost ready!*" Zephyr said.

Facing her party, Zephyr urged them to pick up their pace and ready themselves for the journey.

"Stop staring!" she shouted. "We have to move now!"

Then, when the party was prepared, Zephyr waved goodbye to the talking weeping willows, and she and her friends took off after the silver unicorn.

Although the party couldn't help but gawk and sigh at the unicorn's beauty, they all struggled to keep their wits about themselves.

The silver unicorn made sure to always walk a yard ahead of Zephyr, and silently, Zephyr and her friends tracked the unicorn without knowing where it led them.

Chapter 11

The Cyclopes

The silver unicorn continued to lead Zephyr and her friends forward and through Silveron at a steady pace.

Little Herb pointed out carefully that he thought the unicorn was taking them in the opposite direction from Sandus, though he wasn't completely sure. Then soon, after hours of travel, Zephyr and her friends were wondering how much further the silver unicorn would go before they reached their destination.

But a few more hours later, after following the unicorn for almost an entire day, the creature finally stopped in the midst of the afternoon, and it stood a yard away from Zephyr and waited.

Dismounting Tarn, Zephyr approached the unicorn and spoke.

"Are you stopping to rest?" she asked.

"You may rest if you like," the unicorn told Zephyr. *"I never tire or grow hungry."*

"Oh," Zephyr said with surprise. *"Then, why did you stop?"*

"I felt I should. I always follow my impulses."

"Well, thank you," Zephyr said. *"My friends are probably hungry by now."*

"We can take a break," Zephyr told her party as she turned around.

"Thank goodness," Trinda said with a sigh. "I'm starving!"

She unpacked some Wind Whipped Nimbus Juice and Fluffy Cloud Biscuits, which Master Air Walker had given Zephyr and her friends in Aeria.

"I need time to figure out our location," Little Herb said as he examined his maps. "This is quite a detour."

Settling down, Zephyr and her party relaxed as they ate, drank, and got a little shuteye.

However, after half an hour, Zephyr noticed that the silver unicorn was nowhere to be found, and she jumped up quickly.

"The unicorn!" she said. "It's gone! Where did it go?!"

"Unicorn!" she shouted as she looked about frantically. *"Unicorn! Where are you?!"*

"I'm sure it's probably grazing somewhere nearby," Sir Gallan said.

"It's got to be," Zephyr said.

Together, she and her friends separated and ventured off in different directions as they tried to find the silver unicorn.

But after several minutes of searching, Zephyr and Sir Gallan returned to where they had first stopped.

"It's gone," Zephyr said in a worried tone. "There must be some mistake. It was supposed to lead me to the Sword of Wonders."

"Ahh!" someone suddenly screamed from nearby.

"That sounded like Liz!" Zephyr said fearfully.

Then, a loud roar came from the same place as the scream.

Unsheathing his long broad sword, Sir Gallan rushed towards the source of the noises, and Zephyr hurried after him.

They ran through groups of trees and bushes until they came upon a giant clearing, and what Zephyr saw made her gasp.

In the center of the clearing, Elizabeth Thompson was fighting for her life as she used all the karate techniques she knew and wielded her yellow glowing crystal spear as best she could.

She was battling two cyclopes—sizable creatures with thick bald heads, blood-red skin, dirty black nails, and each with one large red eye in the center of their heads. When they growled and roared, the cyclopes revealed their many sharp pointed teeth like the fangs of a wolf. Also, they wore fur clothing, and they each had huge wooden clubs. And, Zephyr couldn't help but notice a foul odor coming from them and their dirty feet that seemed as though they hadn't been washed in years.

"Help me!" Liz screamed.

She could barely hold off the clubbing attempts of the cyclopes, and the lightning from her spear was useless against them.

Then, in an instant, Liz's spear was knocked a foot away from her, and one of the cyclopes smacked her in the face with the back of his hand, rendering her unconscious. Next, he threw Elizabeth over his shoulder, and Zephyr could see blood dripping from her nose.

Fortunately, however, Sir Gallan was upon the cyclopes in another second, and Zephyr witnessed fine swordsmanship and skill that she had never seen before in her life. Though the cyclopes had defeated Liz, they met their match in the Ruby Knight, Sir Gallan.

The cyclopes had tremendous strength, but Sir Gallan was just as strong, and he was wearing magical armor.

With each of the cyclopes' clubs and hand swings, Sir Gallan met the fatal attempts with blocks from his sword.

Then quickly, he stuck the cyclopes that was carrying Liz in the foot with his weapon, making him jump up and down in pain and lose his balance.

And, as the cyclopes fell, Sir Gallan flipped into the air and landed on his shoulder. Grabbing Liz with his free hand, he jumped away, just as the cyclopes hit the ground.

Next, in the second cyclopes' attempt to kill Sir Gallan, he started swinging his club at him.

But evading the attacks, Sir Gallan moved to the side with Liz, and the second cyclopes ended up clubbing the first one that was still lying on the ground, causing him to roar and growl in agony as he was killed.

Breaking free from simply watching Sir Gallan fight, Zephyr raised her hand and prepared to cast a spell, but she didn't think she needed to, for Sir Gallan was handling the situation perfectly.

As the Ruby Knight laid Liz down carefully, he faced the other cyclopes, and Brandon, Helga, Little Herb, the white centaurs, and the fairy guards finally made it into the clearing to see what was happening.

"I've never seen such monsters!" Helga said loudly as she grabbed onto Zephyr's waist.

"We've got to help!" Brandon said quickly as he held up his crystal sword.

"Wait!" Zephyr said as she raised her hand. "I don't think Sir Gallan needs any help! We'd probably just get in the way!"

And then, everyone saw that Zephyr was correct.

With a sweeping kick, Sir Gallan forced the second cyclops off of his feet, and the creature hit the ground with such a thud that Helga fell backward.

Then, with all his might, Sir Gallan stabbed the cyclopes in the eye with his sword, and that was the end of both monsters.

While he caught his breath, Sir Gallan cleaned his sword and picked up Liz and her crystal spear. And, he carried Liz and her weapon toward Little Herb.

Zephyr noticed that Liz's crystal spear began to glow red in Sir Gallan's hands because his soul catered to fire, and the sight made her think of Cor and the battle raging in Crystotopia.

"That was awesome!" Brandon told Sir Gallan. "You've got to teach me some moves!"

"I believe this young maiden is in need of your services, healer," Sir Gallan told Little Herb as he placed Elizabeth on the ground in front of him.

"I must work fast!" Little Herb said.

Bending over, he dug into his satchel as he searched for healing supplies.

"She has taken quite a blow to the face and has lost a lot of blood," he said. Removing a thick green leafy substance, Little Herb held it over Liz's nose to stop it from bleeding.

"Just a little wrag root," he said. "Thicker than wood, but much softer. I usually use it for bandaging, but it's good for nose bleeds too."

After a few minutes, Elizabeth's nose stopped bleeding, but she was still unconscious.

"Yuck!" Trinda said as she observed the dried blood around Liz's nose. "All that blood makes me queasy!"

"Will she be okay?" Zephyr asked.

"Yes," Little Herb said. "She'll be fine now that the bleeding has stopped. But, she's had the wind knocked out of her. I'm going to mix a mood potion to help her feel better. I have the ingredients for it, but...I haven't mixed one before."

The healer pulled several herbs out of his satchel as well as a mortar and pestle.

"Let me make the potion," Helga said. "All dwarves are known for their potion-making skills. I'll have it done in a jiffy."

However, Little Herb gazed at Helga with unsure eyes.

"It's fine," Zephyr said. "She is excellent at making potions."

So, Little Herb gave Helga the ingredients for the potion and the mortar and pestle reluctantly.

In five minutes, Helga produced an orange potion that smelled and tasted like peaches, and she handed it to Little Herb proudly.

"Impressive!" he said with a smile. "You are good!"

"Typical of a dwarf," Helga said with folded arms.

Little Herb slipped a little of the potion down Liz's throat, and she bolted up immediately.

"Oh," she said with wide eyes. "My head. It hurts. But I feel so...so happy."

"You were knocked out by the cyclopes," Zephyr said. "But Sir Gallan saved you."

Standing, Liz beamed as she gave Sir Gallan a bear hug.

"You saved me!" she said. "Isn't life positively wonderful?!"

"Maybe I overdid it," Helga said with a frown.

"No," Little Herb said. "It's supposed to be strong. It's effective as long as she stays happy and doesn't think about the pain."

"And, we still have lots of potion left," he said as he held up the mortar in which Helga had mixed the mood potion. "I'll just put this in a flask in case we need it later."

Little Herb removed an empty flask and poured the mood potion inside it before he slipped the flask back into his satchel.

Zephyr was happy that Liz was okay, but she still sank to her knees and sighed with despair.

"What's wrong?" Trinda asked her. "You can tell me. Let's talk woman to woman."

"The silver unicorn is gone," Zephyr said. "And, we've only gotten into trouble. Liz could have been killed by those cyclopes! And for what?! We're right back where we started, and I'm so confused!"

"I'm sure that unicorn will be along soon," Trinda said. "It probably ran away because of those monsters."

"You might be right," Zephyr said as she rubbed the crystal ring on her finger. "It will probably come back. But, I think I should check with Scorn to see how the battle is going just in case."

Closing her eyes, Zephyr ran "Sightus Impetus Executo!" through her mind and raised her fingers.

Then, images of the battle in Crystotopia became visible.

"Hello, Scorn," Zephyr thought. *"How is everything?"*

"Not well," Scorn thought as he soared through the air.

Flying closer to the ground, he explained what was happening, and Zephyr could visually understand what was transpiring through Scorn's sight.

"Queen Astra has been injured," Scorn told Zephyr. *"Also, Cor and Ember's army have defeated the white centaurs. But King Jaffa, the Panther King and his army of animal beasts are fighting alongside King Hordas, the Elf King and his elf army to hold Cor off. Apparently, for once, they are getting along."*

Zephyr observed that Cor had started fires everywhere that were ravaging Crystotopia. The animal beasts and the elves were giving their all as they battled Cor and Ember's army of fire creatures and black dragons. And, Zephyr saw in the middle of the battle a giant black panther walking like a person with sparkling diamond eyes that she knew to be King Jaffa. And, fighting beside him with a thin and lanky figure, pine-colored skin, green eyes, a sharp wooden sword, and a leafy green crown on his head, was who Zephyr guessed to be King Hordas. It was amazing because King Hordas and King Jaffa had never gotten along, but now they had joined each other to stand against the Dark Forces.

As Scorn dodged flames and arrows, Zephyr saw fairy guards and sorcerers battling against what she recognized to be King Vigor and his Emerald Knights. Zephyr could tell who King Vigor was because no one fought as fiercely and as tediously as he.

With blood-red eyes, shiny green armor, caramel skin, dirty chestnut hair, and a beard, he was a frightening sight. Also, King Vigor seemed to kill a person each second and was relentless in fighting. It was almost like he lived off of killing others as he did air to breathe.

Then, Zephyr surveyed the battle as she tried to catch sight of her father, and she soon had a clear view of him and Syphron. Her father was fighting with a regular sword and shield with fairy guards, dwarves, and several Ruby Knights by his side. Also, Syphron was leading what looked like the entire Council of Sorcerers to cast spells for attack and defense.

"Father!" Zephyr thought with worry. *"He's still alive, and Syphron too!"*

"Yes," Scorn thought. *"Your father and Syphron are doing well, but the Dark Forces are slowly winning the battle. Also, the healers are busy trying to tend to the wounds of the allied kingdoms' armies."*

As Scorn spoke, Zephyr spotted dozens of blue people dressed in leafy clothing running around the battlefield trying to help injured soldiers.

"And General Bubble Toe and Vainaquia's army are attacking King Trump of Silveron and his forces," Scorn told Zephyr. *"But King Trump would do much better if he would stop looking at his reflection in his sword,"*

Zephyr observed a handsome man with golden skin, thick black hair, and a beard, who was wearing silver armor similar to the rest of his troops. She reasoned that this man was King Trump.

Together, he and his men were trying to ward off the magic and attacks of Vainaquia's army of water wizards and sea creatures.

"And there's Prince Wart and his army," Scorn thought to Zephyr. *"He's attacking Toron's brother, Prince Sardion, and the forces of Sandus."*

And then, Zephyr observed trackers, trolls, and ogres fighting sand creatures as well as warriors wielding sabers. She also saw with golden eyes, sand-colored skin, and pitch-black hair, dressed in golden armor as well as wielding a golden saber, Prince Sardion, who was battling Prince Wart. Prince Sardion resembled Prince Toron greatly and was just as handsome, and Prince Wart was as ugly as always.

Dressed in red armor with oak-colored hair, black eyes, warts covering his face, and tan skin, and armed with a broad sword with a black hilt, Prince Wart was doing his best to defeat Toron's brother.

"There's Queen Lila and Brith's forces," Scorn thought to Zephyr. *"They're attacking King Mourner and the small army of Lamentia. For some reason, King Mourner keeps using magic to make people near him cry so he can catch them off guard. Fortunately, Queen Lila of Brith can blind anyone who looks upon her. So, it's pretty even I guess."*

Zephyr saw fairies, small pixies, and sprites attacking soldiers in black armor. But, she couldn't see Queen Lila clearly, for brilliant and blinding light surrounded her. And, the soldier wearing the fanciest black armor and a crown on his head kept waving his hand as he stood next to his opponents. Then, he would wait until they cried to attack them. With sad black eyes, short orange hair, and mocha skin, Zephyr knew that this soldier in black armor was King Mourner.

"Then," Scorn thought. *"Aeria's forces are battling rebels from Mineralda."*

And as Scorn flew through the sky, Zephyr saw air wizards fighting earth wizards and hordes of dwarves with black pointed hats.

"Thanks for the update, Scorn," Zephyr thought sadly to her falcon. *"Take care of everyone for me. I'll help you somehow."*

"I'll try. Goodbye," Scorn thought to Zephyr.

Zephyr opened her eyes, and she found that her friends were sitting down watching Sir Gallan teach Brandon sword techniques.

"The battle isn't going well," she told her party.

"It's okay, Your Highness," Helga said. "I'm sure everything will work out."

But, Zephyr could see that Helga had doubt written on her face.

"Oh, that stupid unicorn!" Zephyr said angrily. "Where could it have gone off to?"

"Are you referring to me?" someone asked Zephyr.

Turning, she found the silver unicorn standing still just as beautiful as ever.

"You're back!" Zephyr said happily.

She ran to hug the unicorn, but it backed away from her.

"Don't touch me!" the unicorn said.

"I'm...I'm sorry."

"I won't warn you again."

"Where did you go?" Zephyr asked. *"And, where did you come from? I thought you had run away."*

"It doesn't matter. I'm here now. I hope you have rested because we must go."

The unicorn turned around and walked on until it was a yard away from Zephyr. Then, it faced her and waited for her to follow.

"Come on," Zephyr told her friends. "We have to leave. The unicorn is ready."

Zephyr and her party gathered their things as quickly as they could and readied themselves for departure.

Then the unicorn started to lead them again, and they tracked it as best they could.

"I don't have a good feeling about her," Tarn told Zephyr.

"Neither do I," Zephyr replied softly. *"But, I don't have a choice. I must follow her. Otherwise, I would be completely lost."*

"But, we're lost already."

"It's alright. I think the unicorn will help us. At least...I hope it does."

Though conflicted about the trustworthiness of the silver unicorn, Zephyr and her party tried to put their concerns aside. As much as Zephyr disliked the creature, without it, she had no inkling as to the location of the Sword of Wonders. So, she only hoped that she wasn't walking into a trap.

Chapter 12

---◈◈◈---

The Flowers of Sadness

Before Zephyr and her friends knew it, night fell, and they were weary from following the silver unicorn's path. Also, they could hardly see where they were going.

Fortunately, everyone was able to track the silver unicorn for it shimmered and sparkled in the dark. But, this did little to override the fatigue that Zephyr and her friends felt.

Only Sir Gallan, the white centaurs, and the fairy guards had the gall and ability to keep traveling through the night, for they were trained warriors.

"Zephyr," Brandon said with a moan. "I think we should stop. I can barely keep my eyes open."

"Yes, Your Highness," Helga said with a yawn. "Please ask the unicorn if we may rest for the night."

"We can't," Zephyr said with one eye open. "The silver unicorn is still moving. We have to follow...have to keep...going."

Oddly enough, not only was Zephyr tired, but she was starting to feel extremely sad for some reason.

However, in an instant, her eyes forced themselves to close, and Zephyr slumped forward on Tarn's back.

She almost didn't notice when Tarn stopped moving, but Sir Gallan called to her.

"Your Highness," he said as he shook her quickly.

"Huh?!" Zephyr said as she bolted up.

"The unicorn has disappeared again!" Sir Gallan said.

"What?!" Zephyr said, and she was suddenly alert and awake. "What did you say?!"

"The unicorn," Sir Gallan said. "It's gone!"

Zephyr peered about quickly, but she only saw darkness around her, and there was no sign of the silver unicorn.

"It did it again!" she said as she threw up her hands. "Great! Just great! I close my eyes for one second and it vanishes!"

"It will probably come back," Thantos said. "It must disappear as a habit."

"It might have gone to get some shuteye," Trinda said. "This is a good chance for us to get some rest too. We should follow its example and go to sleep. It'll be here in the morning, I'm sure."

"We don't even know where we are or if it is safe to stop here," Zephyr said.

But just as she spoke, a halbert was at her throat, and guards in black armor surrounded her and her friends.

***

"Tell us who you are to trespass on Lord Tear's land!" one guard said loudly.

"Please kind sirs," Sir Gallan said. "We are merely humble travelers making our way."

"Liar!" one of the guards said as he hit Sir Gallan on the head. "We can tell you are a Ruby Knight! Only they wear armor such as yours!"

"We mean no harm," Zephyr said. "Why, if you let us go, we will leave Lord Tear's land immediately."

"Too late for that!" one of the guards said with a laugh. "You'll have to answer to Lord Tear himself! He decides the fate of trespassers!"

"Who is Lord Tear anyway?" Trinda asked.

"Who is Lord Tear!" one of the guards repeated with surprise. "Why he's the most powerful lord in Lamentia, and you are on his land in Depressius, a section of the kingdom."

"Oh!" Zephyr said with a gasp. "We didn't know..."

"Silence! Explain yourself to Lord Tear! We don't want to hear your lies!"

In the blink of an eye, Zephyr and her friends were in gray glowing bonds, and Tarn and the other horses were rounded up. Then, they were all led through the darkness of a forest that encircled them.

It was still late at night, and Zephyr wondered how Lord Tear's guards managed to find her and her friends in the dark.

Together, Zephyr and her party were directed to a giant castle made of gray and black rock and taken inside, and the party's horses were immediately led into a stable in the main courtyard. But, Zephyr and her friends were forced to go further into the castle.

"Shouldn't Lord Tear be asleep at this hour?" Liz asked.

"No," one of the guards answered. "Lord Tear often stays up at night to paint. He always gets bursts of inspiration, and right now, his latest creative spark has been fueled by depression over his late friend."

"That's so sad," Helga said. "His friend died?"

"Actually," one of the guards said. "Lord Tear killed him because he was unhappy and tired of their friendship."

"My goodness!" Helga said with a nervous gulp. "He's quite the character!" Soon, Zephyr and her friends were brought to a pair of magnificent wooden doors carved with elaborate detail and design, and Zephyr reasoned that they were the doors to Lord Tear's throne room. However, Zephyr swore that as she drew closer to the wooden doors she could hear crying coming from behind them.

But oblivious to this fact, the guards knocked on the throne room doors calmly.

"Oh!" a heavy voice called. "Oh, do come in if you must! Ohh!"

The guards opened the doors and dragged Zephyr and her friends inside. But to Zephyr, Lord Tear's throne room was the strangest one she had ever seen, and it was much more like an art studio.

There were paintings and portraits everywhere as well as splattered paint and wooden sculptures. Even Lord Tear's wooden throne was covered with paint as well as a canvas.

And then, there was Lord Tear himself. With long jet-black hair and pecan skin, Lord Tear was dressed in long flowing black garments, and his dark brown eyes were red from crying.

Holding a paintbrush in his hand, he was busy creating what Zephyr guessed to be a portrait of his late friend.

"My Lord," the guards said with a bow as they forced Zephyr and her friends to their knees. "We found these trespassers in the forest."

"Really," Lord Tear said. "How dreadful? How absolutely morbid? Why were they trespassing?"

"They claimed that they were just passing through," one of the guards answered. "But this one here is a Ruby Knight," the guard said as he pointed to Sir Gallan.

"Oh this is terrible news," Lord Tear said as he continued to paint. "Ruby Knights are traitors to the Dark Forces and must be killed. How tragic that you have caught me at such an inopportune moment. I am in mourning you see."

"This guy needs therapy," Trinda whispered. "A lot of it."

"What to do, what to do," Lord Tear said. "You see, I absolutely detest dealing with trespassers. It's quite a putdown actually, and it always ends in death. Not mine of course, though."

"So, you plan to kill us!" Brandon said angrily. "Maybe you would feel better if you let us go!"

"Go?" Lord Tear said with a chuckle. "I wouldn't dare do such a thing, my boy. Obviously, you know nothing of Lamentian philosophy. A true Lamentian must harness their sad feelings and put them to good use. By forcing ourselves into states of utter despair, we can channel our negative energy into amazing artistic expression and enlightenment. So you see, my dear boy, I can't let you go."

"I have an idea," Liz said with clenched teeth. "Why don't you kill yourself?! There's nothing as depressing as that!"

"Mmm," Lord Tear said as he rubbed his chin. "I think you may be on to something my child."

"To be or not to be?" he said as he threw his hand over his face. "That is the question."

"However," Lord Tear said as he cleared his throat. "Although to do myself in would be depressing, and at the same time, I wouldn't be able to be enlightened or express myself creatively. I wouldn't...exist."

"No, my dear," Lord Tear said as he faced Liz. "I'm afraid I can't kill myself. It is you who must die! If I am to reach my own peak of enlightenment and artistic expression, I must be alive to do it! Yes, there have been cases of suicide that sparked sadness and deep thought or creativity in others, but you never hear another peep from the poor dead souls after they are gone. I like it much better if you die! Guards, take them to the pit!"

"No!" Trinda yelled. "I'm too beautiful to be killed!"

Zephyr and her party were carried away back through Lord Tear's castle and into the middle of his main courtyard.

For the first time, Zephyr noticed that in the center of the courtyard, there stood a giant stone structure, which looked like a well. But, as Zephyr drew closer to it, she realized that it was a deep pit.

Then, she and her friends were thrown inside the pit, and their weapons and belongings were tossed in after them.

"Zephyr!" Trinda said with gritted teeth.

"Yes?" Zephyr asked.

"I think that unicorn is a demon in disguise! We're about to die!"

"It's okay," Zephyr said. "I'll get us out of here somehow. I promise."

"At least, I'll try," she said with a gulp.

"Are you comfortable?!" Lord Tear yelled from above. "I hope you aren't!"

Holding several giant blue flowers over the pit, Lord Tear shook them roughly. And then, yellow pollen from the flowers fell into the pit slowly and covered Zephyr and her friends.

"ACHOO!" Helga sneezed suddenly.

"What is that?!" she asked. "It's making my allergies act up!"

"I know what it is," Little Herb said with a sigh. "It's the secret behind the unbearable sadness that afflicts those who enter Lamentia."

"The secret?" Zephyr repeated with awe.

"You see," Little Herb explained. "Lamentia is the one place on Danus where a certain rare blue flower grows. Every healer knows that its scientific name is Lamentia Floralius. But, it is commonly called the flower of sadness. The flowers are spread out everywhere in the kingdom, and their pollen makes whoever comes near it become overwhelmed by grief. Most people know nothing about it and become victims of the flowers' pollen if they enter Lamentia."

"But, why is Lord Tear using the pollen on us?" Zephyr asked.

"I'm sure he is planning to make us so sad that we will hurt each other," Sir Gallan said. "Or ourselves."

"That's ridiculous!" Trinda said. "That flower pollen can't be that potent!"

"Well, I'm not waiting around here to find out," Zephyr said.

Closing her eyes, she focused on her bonds and Wind Chaser, which Lord Tear's guards had tossed into the pit.

Then, Wind Chaser took off and cut through Zephyr's bonds.

"There," she said happily as she stood. "I'll have us out of here in a jiffy."

She started to untie her friends, starting with Trinda first.

"Now, if I can just cast a wind spell to get us out of...."

But, Zephyr fell silent as Trinda hit her in the head with her bow.

"Shut up!" Trinda said as she sobbed. "I'm tired of hearing you babble! Why can't you listen to my problems?!"

"How dare you?!" Zephyr said as she stood with tears in her eyes. "You're so selfish and self-centered! All you care about is yourself!"

"Oh!" Helga wailed. "To think that I gave up my Gusto just to follow some stupid princess who is leading us to our doom!"

"This is so sad!" Sir Gallan said as he sniffled and wiped his eyes. "I'm supposed to die in battle! Not with some squawking children!"

"Children!" Brandon said angrily. "Who are you calling a child?! I'm just as good a warrior as you!"

As Brandon started swinging his crystal sword, it clashed with Sir Gallan's sword and it splashed water everywhere.

"Put a sock in it!" Peantos said. "I'm tired of taking orders from you saps!"

"You know," Trion said as he held his head. "I've just about had it up to the upper part of my body with you fairies!"

In an instant, all of Zephyr's party was fighting and yelling amongst themselves—everyone, except for Elizabeth Thompson.

"Wait!" she said loudly as she flailed her arms. "Stop fighting! It's the sadness taking you guys over! You have to stop it!"

"Be quiet!" Zephyr yelled.

She waved her hand quickly, and a heavy wind blew Liz against the wall of the pit.

"Ow!" Liz yelled as she felt her back in pain. "If you keep this up, you'll kill each other!"

The entire party was in utter chaos, and for a second Liz didn't know what to do. As her friends tried to murder each other, she watched with disbelief. But then, she felt that she had to take action.

"I won't let you hurt each other if it's the last thing I do!" she said loudly.

Standing, she took her yellow glowing crystal spear and twirled it in the air. Then, bringing it down, Liz jabbed it into the ground of the pit lightly, and a small of amount of electricity surged through everyone.

"Hey!" Trinda said. "Can't you see I'm depressed?! What's wrong with you?!" But Liz didn't answer. Instead, she jabbed the ground lightly several more times to shock her friends with electricity and made sure not to electrocute them enough to harm them.

126

Liz didn't stop until almost all of her friends were unconscious, and only Sir Gallan remained standing.

"You!" Sir Gallan said with red puffy eyes. "You're ruining my life! But, you're no match for my armor! It's magic proof you brat, and you're little lightning spear can't do a thing to me!"

"You saved my life, Sir Gallan," Liz said as she took a defensive stance with her spear. "Now, it's my turn to save yours."

Motioning her hand at Sir Gallan, she beckoned and dared him to attack her.

"I'll get you!" Sir Gallan yelled.

Then, he charged at Liz in a wild rage.

If the Ruby Knight had attacked Elizabeth feeling like himself, she would have been no match for his combat art.

But, Sir Gallan was emotional and confused, and Liz knew that she could use his lack of focus and direction to her advantage.

As Sir Gallan charged at her, she sideswiped him and hit him in the back of his head with the blunt end of her spear, knocking him out, and she sighed with relief.

But, even though she had rendered her friends unconscious, she had no idea how to keep them from hurting each other once they awakened.

"Goodness gracious!" Lord Tear called from above.

Apparently, he and his guards had been watching Elizabeth and her friends fight. "You are quite the warrior aren't you?!" he said.

"Are your friends dead?!" he asked. "I don't see any blood!"

As Elizabeth peered up, she realized that Lord Tear thought she was under the influence of the flowers of sadness and that she had killed her friends.

"Yes!" she said as she pretended to cry. "My friends are dead! What have I done?!"

"Well, you have to die too of course," Lord Tear said. "It's only natural. This is quite a tragedy. Quite the tragedy indeed."

"Perhaps, we should shoot her with an arrow, My Lord," one of the guards suggested.

"An arrow!" Liz said with a whimper. "An arrow would not suffice for what I have done to my friends! No, I must die by my own hand!"

Holding up her spear, Liz pointed the tip of it at her chest.

"I take my life now as I see that without my friends, I have no will to live!" she said.

Then, Liz jabbed her spear at herself and yelled.

"Oh!" she said as she bent over and fell forward. "My friends, I shall now join you in death!"

Next, Elizabeth closed her eyes and remained still.

"What a sight!" Lord Tear said as he sobbed.

One of his guards gave him a handkerchief, and he blew his nose.

"This is so terrible and...so inspiring," he said. "I think I'll go paint for a whole day."

"Let them lay there until morning," he told his guards. "Then, you may clean out the pit. I want them to stay there like that for a while. So peaceful."

"Yes, My Lord," the guards said together.

And, after a moment, they all left.

When they were gone, Elizabeth Thompson turned on her side and stood as she raised her spear.

Truthfully, she hadn't stabbed herself at all, and she only pretended that she had done so. Really, Elizabeth had slipped the tip of her spear under her arm to only act like she had taken her life so she could throw off Lord Tear and his guards.

But now, she pondered what she was to do when her friends woke up because she knew that they were still going to be influenced by the pollen of the flowers of sadness. So, Elizabeth started to pace as she entered deep thought.

"Think Liz, think!" she told herself. "Why didn't the pollen affect you?! What makes you different from the others?! There must be some reason! Something that happened to you and didn't happen to everyone else! But, the only thing different...well, I got attacked by the cyclopes!"

No!" she said as threw her hands up with frustration. "That doesn't make any sense!"

Just then, Liz realized that Little Herb was starting to wake up.

"No not yet!" she said. "I still need to figure out how to help you!"

Approaching Little Herb, Liz hit him on the head with the blunt end of her spear, knocking him out once more.

However, as Elizabeth took a step back, she slipped and fell.

Turning, she tried to see what she had tripped over, and she saw that it was the strap of Little Herb's satchel and that her foot had gotten caught in it.

"Stupid bag!" she said. "Not now! I'm brainstorming!"

As Liz tried to shake her leg loose from Little Herb's satchel, a flask of orange liquid rolled out.

"What's this?!" she asked herself as she held up the flask.

Uncorking it, she sniffed the liquid inside.

"This smells like peaches!" she said. "This is the potion that Little Herb gave me after I was attacked by the cyclopes!"

"Wait a minute!" Liz said as her eyes widened with awe. "This potion must have negated the side effects of the flowers of sadness' pollen! I drank this, and the others didn't! Eureka!"

Holding up the potion triumphantly, Liz moved as fast as she could as she slipped some of it into the mouths of her friends, and fortunately, there was just enough to give everyone a sip.

Then, in an instant, everyone was awake, and they seemed like they were back to normal.

"What's going on?!" Zephyr asked as she held her head. "I felt so awful a moment ago! There was so much pain and sadness!"

"The potion Little Herb gave me!" Liz said excitedly. "It was still working on me when Lord Tear sprinkled the flowers of sadness' pollen on us! It kept me from getting so sad and depressed!"

It was the mood potion I made!" Helga said. "We still had some leftovers! So, the pollen and the mood potion must have canceled each other out!"

"Thank you, Lady Elizabeth," Sir Gallan said in a guilty tone. "That was a terrible state I was in. I feel so bad about what I said. You have saved us all fair maiden."

"I never want to see you guys act like that again!" Liz said as she hugged Sir Gallan.

"Let's cut the chit-chat!" Zephyr said. "We've got to get out of this place!"

Taking her spell-casting stance, she thought, "Galeus Maximus Executo!" and as she waved her hand, gusts of wind surrounded her and her friends and carried the whole party out of the pit and into the courtyard above.

"Quick," Sir Gallan said in a whisper. "Get to the stable. The centaurs, the fairy guards, and I will make clear the way."

Together, the fairy guards and the white centaurs nodded at each other and at Sir Gallan, and they all took off together as they ran towards the front gates of Lord Tear's castle.

Meanwhile, Zephyr and her friends ran into the stable to retrieve their horses and to ready them for departure.

"Zephyr!" Tarn said happily as Zephyr unlocked her stall and led her outside. *"What happened?!"*

"You don't want to know," Zephyr said. *"It's too depressing, and I mean that literally."*

As Zephyr and her friends left the stable with the horses, Sir Gallan, the white centaurs, and the fairy guards hurried towards them.

"Come on," Sir Gallan said. "We've taken care of the guards at the castle entrance and opened the gates. But, more will be along soon."

"Right!" Zephyr said.

As she and her party mounted their horses and the white centaurs, they galloped away as fast as they could and out of Lord Tear's castle. And, Peantos, Reen, and Thantos flew behind them.

Zephyr and her friends didn't know where they were going, and they were too afraid of what dangers waited for them elsewhere in Depressius. So, they kept traveling until morning.

Then, they stopped in the thick of a valley that was filled with batches of blue flowers of sadness.

And, as Zephyr and her friends rested, Little Herb and Helga mixed a new batch of mood potion—enough to last for a few days. To be cautious, they gave everyone a second dose of the potion and distributed a first dose to the horses.

That was mainly because Zephyr had pointed out that she thought the horses were getting sad because Tarn kept reminiscing about her old stable in Crystotopia.

Zephyr was grateful to have escaped from Lord Tear, but Trinda Temple and Brandon revealed something that she was very afraid to consider and realize.

"That unicorn is evil!" Trinda said. "It keeps disappearing right before we get attacked, and I know it's doing it on purpose!"

"Yeah!" Brandon said. "What is with that?! That unicorn definitely has it in for us! What if it really isn't the silver unicorn but is some type of shapeshifter or something?!"

"That's a silly notion," Thantos said with a laugh.

"He's right," Zephyr said. "No, I think the unicorn is safe. No one ever said that following it would be easy."

However, Zephyr sighed with doubt for she truly didn't know if the silver unicorn was to be trusted.

"I don't know," Liz said. "I definitely think there is more to it. Maybe the unicorn is testing us somehow."

"I would have to agree," Thantos said. "The silver unicorn is probably a creature that favors no one. It makes sense that for it to lead someone to the Sword of Wonders, the person would have to go through a series of trials. Better yet, maybe as the guardian of the sword, the silver unicorn might be trying to protect it."

"Fascinating," Elizabeth said as she rubbed her chin. "That makes sense. Following the unicorn probably leads to the sword, but with the unicorn, its duty to protect the sword must make sure that whoever seeks it is worthy of its power. It must be impartial. It has to guard the Sword of Wonders and favor no one to have it. Only those who prove themselves can attain it, no matter how much the unicorn likes or dislikes the candidate. It's perfectly clear now."

"Yeah right!" Trinda said. "I know a trickster when I see one! I should because I'm one myself! I'm beautiful and appealing on the outside, but I have my own interests at heart."

"Is that what reasoning you use to control the school?!" Zephyr said with a grin, and Trinda shot her a cold glare.

But just then, a heavy wind blew, and Zephyr and her friends grew silent for the wind seemed unnatural.

Then, in the distance, the silver unicorn appeared once more, but Zephyr wasn't happy to see it.

In fact, she was downright suspicious and angry as she wondered if the unicorn would lead her and her friends into more trouble. However, she knew that only time possessed the answer she sought.

Chapter 13

---◆◇◆---

The Nymph Sisters

"*H*ello unicorn," Zephyr said cautiously. "*Funny how you disappear when we get into trouble and show up later. And, following you hasn't taken us to the Sword of Wonders yet. Are you ready to lead us into even more fatal situations?*"

"*Do not mock me, child!*" the silver unicorn said. "*My actions need no explanation. You don't have to follow me if you don't want to do so, but I am your only chance of finding the sword.*"

"*How do I know that I can believe that?*" Zephyr asked. "*I can't tell if you are helping us find the sword or trying to get rid of us.*"

"*There is no time to argue. I won't answer your questions. I'm leaving, and it is your choice to follow me or go your own way.*"

Turning, the unicorn started to walk away.

"Oh!" Zephyr said loudly. "This is so frustrating! Come on everyone!"

"Your Highness," Helga said. "Is it still safe to go after the creature?"

"I don't know," Zephyr said. "But, I have no choice. Stay and go back to Crystotopia if you like, but I'm going to see where this unicorn takes me."

"I'd love to leave!" Trinda said eagerly.

"Then, you will return to Crystotopia without me," Liz said. "I'm not giving up, and I vote that we follow the unicorn."

"As scared as I am," Helga said. "My duty is to the Princess. I...I trust her judgment. At least I think I do."

"Fine!" Trinda said as she rolled her eyes. "I can see where this is going."

Zephyr and her party gathered themselves and hurried after the silver unicorn, though the heroes were much more alert than they had previously been.

However, traveling through Lamentia was easy with the help of Little Herb and Helga's mood potion. The pollen from the blue flowers of sadness had no effect on Zephyr and her friends any longer. And, the silver unicorn stayed off of the main roads and areas filled with Lamentians, who would oppose Zephyr and her friends.

So, before long, the silver unicorn led Zephyr and her party out of Lamentia, and Zephyr could tell that she and her friends had left the depressing kingdom when instead of fields of blue flowers and green trees, they were environed by white trees with golden leaves as well as pools of golden liquid.

Also, tiny white lights filled the air as well as slightly larger blue ones. One of the blue lights flew in front of Trinda's face, and she could see that it was actually a tiny person with wings and wearing silver clothing.

"Wow!" Trinda said. "A tiny person that can fly."

"Pixies," Reen said. "We're in Brith. It's the kingdom of origin for all fairies, pixies, nymphs, and sprites."

"I remember seeing a pixy in Fruitonia," Liz said. "But, there are so many here."

"Yes," Zephyr whispered. "And it's so beautiful and bright."

Just then, the silver unicorn stopped and faced her, and Zephyr told Tarn to stay still.

"Why are we stopping?" Brandon asked. "Are we there?"

"I don't know," Zephyr said.

After a minute, the silver unicorn threw up its front legs and took off past a group of trees.

"Hey!" Zephyr yelled.

"Hurry Tarn!" she told her horse. *"Catch up with the unicorn!"*

Taking off, Tarn ran as fast as she could, and Zephyr soon spotted the silver unicorn in the distance, and her horse was gaining on her.

But, just as the silver unicorn made an abrupt turn, and Tarn followed her, the horse came upon a giant golden river.

Skidding as she attempted to stop, Tarn accidentally propelled Zephyr forward into the depths of the river, and Elizabeth fell off Tarn's back and hit the ground.

"Zephyr!" Liz called as she scrambled to her feet.

However, there was no trace of her, and in another second, the rest of the party caught up to Liz and Tarn.

"What happened?" Sir Gallan asked.

"Zephyr fell in the river!" Liz said. "She's under the water!"

"This is terrible!" Helga said with a gasp.

"We've got to go in after her!" Sir Gallan said. "But with my armor on, I'll sink to the bottom of the river. Can one of you do it?"

"I'll go!" Brandon said boldly.

Then, without another word, he jumped into the river, and the party waited for him to surface again. However, there was no sign of Brandon or Zephyr.

"There's something strange about that river," Liz said. "We can't keep jumping into it. We may never come out."

"I have an idea," Trinda said. "Do any of you have any rope?"

"Yes," Little Herb said as he reached into his satchel. "But, it's a special rope used to stop the flow of blood in the arms or the legs."

"Give it to me," Trinda said.

Little Herb gave Trinda the rope, and she tied one end of it to one of the arrows from her quill.

"Now," she said. "One of you can go into the river and hold onto this arrow. If you don't come out, we can pull you out with the rope."

"I'll try," Peantos said as he took the arrow. "Can't fly until my wings are dry though."

Trinda gave the other end of the rope to Sir Gallan, and taking a deep breath, Peantos threw himself into the river as the rope attached to Trinda's arrow started to move slowly into the water as well.

"He's going pretty deep," Trion said as he watched the rope Sir Gallan held slip further into the river. And, soon, he motioned to Sir Gallan.

"He should be at the river's bottom by now!" he said loudly. "You should pull him up, or he'll run out of air!"

Stepping back, Sir Gallan used all of his strength to pull on the rope, but the rope wouldn't budge and started to drag him into the water.

"Ugh!" he said with a grunt. "He...he must have a good grip!"

Slowly, Sir Gallan's feet started to slide towards the river.

"Let us help you!" Trion said. "Come on centaurs!"

Together, Trion, Cara, Piro, and Valon grabbed Sir Gallan's waist as they tried to help him tug on the rope.

Yet, although they gained some leeway, in an instant, they all started sliding into the river.

"Hey!" Liz said. "Hold on!"

She, Trinda, Helga, Reen, and Thantos grabbed the centaurs and the rope as they also pulled.

However, the entire party was yanked into the river, and as they still held onto the rope and each other, they plummeted and were sucked deeper into the water, until they reached the river's bottom.

But much to their surprise, they seemed to fall out of the bottom of the golden river, and they landed on a dry rocky surface below.

"What...where are we?" Liz asked.

Peering up, she observed that the river's water was moving about and was full of colorful fish, but it was suspended in the air above where she was standing. Wherever Elizabeth was happened to be bare and dry, and just ahead, there was a large cave, from which a light was shining.

"I'm about to find out where we are," Sir Gallan said. "But, stay here! It might be dangerous!"

Moving forward, he approached the cave before him cautiously with his sword poised for attack.

And, as he drew closer to the cave, he noticed uncontrollable laughs and giggles coming from inside.

Then, just as Sir Gallan reached the cave entrance, a stream of water surrounded him and swept him into the cave.

"Sir Gallan!" Trinda called.

"Look Estuary!" someone from inside the cave said loudly. "It's another one, and he's cute! Oh, and there might be more guests at the entrance! I'll go check!"

Suddenly, a stream of water trickled out of the cave and sped towards the rest of the party outside.

"Watch out!" Trinda screamed. "Keep away from the water!"

But, before the rest of Zephyr's friends could escape, water in the shape of vines snatched them and carried them into the cave.

"No!" Helga screamed. "Let me go!"

"Do calm down," a high-pitched voice said with a laugh. "So feisty!"

Inside, the cave actually looked like the interior of a small house with stone tables and chairs as well as two beds.

Zephyr, Sir Gallan, Brandon, and Peantos were sitting in several chairs, and what looked like chains made of water bound their hands to the chairs' sides.

But then, the rest of the party was forced to sit in chairs and were bound by more watery chains.

"I see they got to you too," Zephyr told her friends.

"What is going on?" Trinda asked.

"We're having a party," someone said in an unusual voice.

All of a sudden, Trinda gasped as streams of water transformed and took on the shape of two women, except their bodies and faces were made of water. Also, one woman was very chubby while the other was amazingly thin.

"Nymphs," Reen said with a sigh. "I should have known. They live all over Brith, and these two must be water nymphs that live in this river."

"Very good," the thin nymph said. "I'm glad we got that cleared up. I'm Estuary."

"And this," she said as she pointed to the larger nymph. "This is my sister, Lagoonia, and you all are our new guests and best friends!"

"If we are your guests and friends," Zephyr said. "Then why are you keeping us here by force? Can't you free our arms?"

"Oh no," Lagoonia said as she shook her head. "We can't do that! You see, my sister and I hardly ever get any visitors. We used to entertain people regularly. But after a while, people stopped coming. So..."

"Yes," Estuary continued. "So, we decided to make anyone who came to visit us stay as long as we could keep them."

"How long would that be?" Helga asked fearfully.

"As long as you can survive on water," the nymphs answered together. "Most people can live on liquids for a couple of weeks."

"You mean to tell me you don't have any food?!" Trinda said with disbelief. "That's horrible!"

"Oh no it's quite true," Lagoonia said. "Just look at what's left of our other visitors."

The nymph pointed behind her to a pile of skeletons and bones in the corner of the house.

"They were here a few years ago!"

"That's awful!" Liz said.

"Get me out of here!" Trinda screamed. "I'm not going to sit here till I die!"

She struggled with her chains, but it was no use.

"Stop fighting us," Estuary said with a giggle. "Remember, you are our guests. So, we want to have some fun with you while we can."

"What's a nymph anyway?" Brandon asked angrily.

"It's a spirit of nature," Liz explained. "I knew they were playful because of my studies of mythology, but this is just downright ridiculous."

"What to do, what to do," Estuary said as she rubbed her chin.

"I know sister!" Lagoonia said excitedly. "We should have a tea party!"

"That's a lovely idea!" Estuary said. "Let's prepare right now!"

Estuary aimed her fingers at Zephyr and her friends, and streams of water pulled their chairs around a stone table.

Then, Lagoonia pointed her hands at the table, and teacups and saucers made of water appeared.

"They have amazing control over the element of water!" Liz said with awe.

"Quiet!" Estuary said. "Wait until we speak to you!"

Clearing her throat, she spoke loudly.

"My dear guests!" she said. "Thank you for joining my sister and me in our quaint home. We are gathered here to celebrate life and enjoy each other."

"Now," Estuary said as she nodded at Zephyr. "Would you like some tea dear?"

"I don't have time for...." Zephyr started to say.

But, before she could finish speaking, she got a mouthful of water.

"I'm sorry, you'll have to speak up," Lagoonia said. "We can't quite hear you."

Together, the nymph sisters broke into cackles and boisterous laughter.

Then, Estuary and Lagoonia pointed to the cups on the table as they filled each one magically with water, and the sisters held up the cups in front of them.

"Let us make a toast," Lagoonia said. "A toast to life! Long live our new friends!" The nymph sisters tapped their cups together, and streams of water in the form of hands and arms took turns smacking Zephyr and her friends' cups together as well to join in the toast since they couldn't even move their hands.

And, as Zephyr and her friends tried to protest, they all got mouthfuls of water as their teacups were forced to their lips.

However, Trinda spit out the water from her cup defiantly.

"How rude!" Estuary said. "Where are your manners?! This is a social party!"

"Oh believe me!" Trinda said angrily. "I'm an aristocrat! I know what manners are! But, while we're on the subject, it's the rudest act in the world to force someone to stay in a place like this until they die!"

"Well, I...how dare you?!" Lagoonia said as she put her hands on her hips.

"You see sister," she said as she faced Estuary. "You show people some hospitality, and this is how they repay you."

"Why can't you enjoy your tea?" she asked Trinda.

"It isn't even tea!" Brandon said. "It's just water! Stop playing games!"

"You know what Estuary," Lagoonia said. "I don't like our guests. They aren't very nice at all."

"I agree sister," Estuary said. "Perhaps letting them talk was a hasty decision. I think we should make them be quiet for a while. Maybe that will teach them some respect."

"No!" Zephyr said as she shook her head. "Please, I'm sorry. My friends and I are just...just tired. We will be kind from now on."

"What are you doing?" Liz asked Zephyr in a whisper.

"I'm trying to get us out of this mess," Zephyr replied. "I don't know how yet, but I don't think we should make them angry. They're each very powerful, and there are two of them. Do you have any ideas about how we can escape?"

"No," Liz said. "But you're the sorceress. Can't you think of something?"

"Sorry," Zephyr said. "Together, those two seem unstoppable. Any spell I would cast would be met by potent water magic from each of them. If there were only one of them…"

"Mmm," Liz said. "Perhaps, we won't have to face either of them."

"Come again?" Zephyr said.

"It seems like these sisters are invincible 'together.' But, if they work against each other, I wonder what might happen. We have to figure out what differences they have and use them to make Lagoonia and Estuary turn their magic against each other."

While Zephyr talked to Elizabeth, the nymph sisters were too busy discussing what they were going to do with Zephyr and her friends to notice.

"What differences?" Zephyr said. "Both of them are water nymphs, and they are both silly."

"Well, I think the thin one is attractive," Brandon said. "What's her name again?"

"Estuary," Trinda said in an annoyed tone. "Stop looking at them, Brandon!"

"Wait a second," Liz said. "You may be on to something, Brandon."

"What?!" Trinda said.

"Not now, Trinda," Liz said. "I mean a way to get to the sisters. One of them is skinny, and the other is fat. Plus, they are both very silly. Brandon, you're a guy. Try and give Estuary a compliment. And Sir Gallan, you compliment Lagoonia."

"What good will that do?" Brandon asked.

"Trust me," Liz said.

Sighing, Brandon cleared his throat.

"Excuse me, um...Estuary," he said.

"Yes," the nymph answered as she turned around.

"Has anyone ever told you how beautiful you are?" Brandon said reluctantly. "You're so thin, shapely, and...and fluid-like."

"Oh," Estuary said with a giggle. "That's very kind."

Approaching Brandon, she ran her fingers through his curly hair.

"Do go on," she said. "I haven't received a compliment in ages."

"Well, he already gave you one," Lagoonia said as she pushed her sister out of the way.

"Now," she told Brandon. "Tell me how attractive 'I' am."

Brandon was about to give Lagoonia a compliment when he saw Liz shaking her head signaling for him not to do so.

"No," he said with a gulp.

"What did you say?!" Lagoonia asked in an angry tone.

"No," Brandon repeated nervously. "I'm...I'm only attracted to Estuary."

"Her!" Lagoonia said loudly. "How can you only be attracted to her?! You need a thick woman who can offer you more. I have more matter and body to work with."

"Excuse me?!" Estuary said with rage. "Why can't you just accept that he's attracted to me Lagoonia?! He likes the thin and voluptuous type!"

Shaking her hips, Estuary pushed her hand through her hair, which splashed droplets of water on Brandon.

"He doesn't like chunky beef," she said.

"Chunky beef!" Lagoonia said with a gasp. "You have some nerve!"

As Liz looked at Sir Gallan, she winked at him, and Sir Gallan nodded.

"Lagoonia!" he called. "My lovely buttercup. You are the fairest nymph I have ever seen. Don't worry about your thin sister. I personally love the thickness of your...your caboose. Estuary is the one who would do better to eat something once in a while. She'll make herself sick if she doesn't carry more water."

"See!" Lagoonia said happily as she threw her hand in her sister's face. "He likes my caboose, and he's better looking than that scrawny boy."

"Are you insulting my admirer because he likes me and not you?!" Estuary said. "You're so jealous, Lagoonia! It's flowing all over your face!"

Then suddenly, Lagoonia pointed her hand at Estuary, producing a wave that knocked her against the wall.

"Big mistake!" Estuary screamed as she faced her sister.

And, in an instant, the sisters were at each other's throats rolling on the ground and fighting as they splashed water around the cave.

"I'm going to blow you up!" Estuary yelled.

"Not if I do it first!" Lagoonia screamed.

The water nymphs turned into puddles and reformed their bodies several feet apart from each other.

Then, Estuary threw her hand at her sister first, but Lagoonia was quick to wave her hand at Estuary as well.

Together, the sisters grunted, and their hands trembled as they fought each other with their powers.

And suddenly, the sisters screamed simultaneously, and they were blown apart as water flew into the air. The nymph sisters were so scattered that their remains drizzled all over the cave.

But, also scattered, was the nymphs' magic. And, the chains that held Zephyr and her friends, the teacups, and even the saucers on the table, lost their solid watery shapes and sank to the floor as puddles.

"Get us out of here, Zephyr!" Trinda said as she stood. "I have a feeling those nymphs aren't going to be happy when they get themselves together!"

"Those stone seats weren't meant for centaurs," Cara said as she stretched her legs. "I don't think I'll ever go in another river again after this."

Zephyr's party ran out of the cave, and they faced the river above them anxiously.

"Hold your breath!" Zephyr told her friends.

Then, as they did as Zephyr instructed, she thought, "Waveus Maximus Executo!" and raised her fingers.

A magnificent wave of water surrounded Zephyr and her friends, and using all of her concentration, Zephyr directed the wave to carry everyone through the river above and to the water's surface. Zephyr and her party held their breath until they were tossed out of the river and onto the ground above.

"Whoa!" Brandon said. "That was like a roller-coaster!"

"There you are," Tarn told Zephyr happily. *"I was about to go in after you."* Zephyr laughed as she rubbed the horse's mane.

"Okay," Trinda said. "Now, we know not to go in the water. Let's find a way across the river."

So, it was fortune that favored Zephyr and her friends, and that led them to escape from the clutches of the sister nymphs, Estuary, and Lagoonia. But they were afraid to stay by the river and wait for the silver unicorn to return for fear of the water nymphs. Instead, they found a strip of land leading across the river, and they traveled deeper into the kingdom of Brith.

Chapter 14

The Tree of Life

"BOOM!" everyone heard as thunder ripped through the sky, and Zephyr and her friends bolted up alert and in fear, and the horses moved about uneasily.

"What was that?!" Trinda asked.

"It's only thunder," Valon answered. "Nothing much. I've seen worse with the snowstorms in Glacionus."

"Oh," Trinda said with a sigh of relief.

She was about to try and go back to sleep, when lightning flashed through the sky, and with boisterous thunder, the lightning crackled as it struck a tree branch right above Zephyr's head.

"Watch out, Your Highness!" Sir Gallan yelled, and just before the branch crushed Zephyr, Sir Gallan knocked her out of the way as the branch fell on him instead.

"No!" Helga screamed.

"Let's go!" Trion yelled as he waved to the white centaurs.

Together, he, Cara, Valon, and Piro lifted the branch off of Sir Gallan, and Little Herb ran to the Ruby Knight's side. Zephyr couldn't tell how bad it was, but she sensed that Sir Gallan had been severely injured.

"Maybe I haven't seen worse," Valon said.

"This is no normal storm," Liz said as she narrowed her eyes and peered into the sky.

And as Zephyr looked into the sky, she gasped nervously.

Storm clouds were racing, and lightning was striking in various places at once with thunder so loud and powerful that it shook the ground. Then, heavy rains started to pour.

"What's happening?!" Trinda said. "It's like the end of the world!"

"This is too much action!" Brandon said. "Even for me!"

"Is this a monsoon?!" Liz said as she covered her head with her hands to shield herself from the rain.

"More like a hurricane!" Zephyr said.

Suddenly, winds poured around Zephyr and her friends—winds so strong that Helga was swept off of her feet.

"Oh, Your Highness!" Helga called. "What could be the cause of this?!"

"I know where we can find shelter, Your Highness!" Peantos said as he ran over to Zephyr.

"Take us there!" Thantos said. "We've got to get the Princess to safety!"

"Come!" Thantos told Zephyr as he took her arm. "We can't stay here! We need to get you out of the storm!"

"Right!" Zephyr yelled.

Then, she motioned to Trinda, Brandon, Elizabeth, and Helga.

"Go!" Cara said. "We'll catch up soon enough, and we'll take care of the horses!" Zephyr, Trinda, Liz, Brandon, and Helga took off with the fairy guards, Peantos, Thantos, and Reen as they all held hands.

Zephyr could barely see where she was going, but she tried her best to follow the fairy guards and hold on tightly to her friends.

But suddenly, a small twister appeared in the middle of Zephyr's path, and she and her friends were tossed about as the twister hurled them into the air.

"Helga!" Zephyr yelled.

She struggled to keep her grip on her nursemaid's hand.

"No!" Helga yelled. "Don't let go!"

However, slowly, Zephyr was torn from Helga and forced into the sky.

Screaming, she was sure she was going to die, and soon she found herself plummeting.

Yet, mysteriously, Zephyr began to float and descend with ease until her feet touched the ground gently and she was safe.

Wherever she was, the storm did not touch, though she could hear it raging on in other parts of Brith.

As Zephyr tried to get her bearings, she saw that she was in the middle of a clearing in a wood, where there were trees so thick and large that she couldn't have possibly entered or left the clearing by traveling on foot.

Glancing down, Zephyr saw that the ground was covered with moss as well as golden lilies, and tiny bright yellow sparkling lights swirled in the air of the clearing. Also, Zephyr felt oddly serene and calm.

However, as Zephyr turned, what she saw next shocked her deeply.

She noticed that behind her in the center of the wood and clearing, there sat a tree so thick, tall, and magnificent that Zephyr got dizzy trying to take all of it in. But, the strangest thing about the tree was that it did not seem to be made of regular wood and leaves.

Instead, it was a metal tree whose bark Zephyr guessed to be silver. Also, the tree's leaves were unusual as well, and as Zephyr drew closer, she realized that they were sparkling rubies.

Just as Zephyr was about to touch the tree, a peculiar wind blew behind her, and she turned to find the silver unicorn watching her.

"Hello, Zephyr," the unicorn said.

As it walked towards her, Zephyr noticed that the unicorn's silver horn was glowing a luminescent gold.

"Silver unicorn," Zephyr said. *"Have you come to take me on another wild goose chase?"*

"No," the unicorn replied. *"Your journey ends here. I shall take you no further."*

"What are you saying?" Zephyr asked with wide eyes.

"This, Princess, is the birthplace of the Sword of Wonders. The tree in the middle of this wood, with bark of silver and leaves of rubies, was the tree from which the sword was made. It is the Tree of Life, and it contains a magic—a force which governs me as well as you. The tree is as old as me, and it will live as long as I shall live. At the beginning of time and Danus, the tree was a gift to this world. Without its presence, our world would not exist."

"What?" Zephyr said as she held her chest with awe.

"Ages ago," the silver unicorn said. *"This world's creator made this tree and sealed his power within it. From the tree's magic, life blossomed and flourished on this planet. Eventually, life on Danus grew more complex, and the people were given the freedom of choice. The creator knew this would be. So, he used one of the Tree of Life's branches to fashion a weapon. It was a sword, and because it came from the Tree of Life, it also contained the*

creator's powers. The sword is a test, and with each century's new generation, the people decide whether they will use the sword's abilities for good or evil. If the people fail the test, they will use the sword for evil, and the world will eventually be destroyed, proving that the creator was mistaken in giving people the freedom of choice and lending them his power. But if the sword is used for good, the world will grow fuller, and richer, and shall flourish. However, only one and his bloodline is chosen each century to wield the sword—one who passes all the necessary tests and who possesses the potential to use the sword for good. But, the decision to use the sword for good or evil belongs to only the chosen and his bloodline."

"I don't understand," Zephyr said as she shook her head. *"Where is the sword? The tree is here, but I don't see the sword."*

"Only I can make the sword appear," the unicorn said. *"The sword is held by the Tree of Life's roots hidden beneath the ground, but I alone have the ability to summon it, and then the first person who touches the sword, may claim it. You, Princess, are fortunate to even be here in the presence of the Tree of Life. Its location is secret and magically hidden. It is only visible and within reach when I make it so. But I only do that when one who is pure of heart and brave proves himself worthy of the final test. Princess, it was you alone who were to be tested. That was why I used my magic to make a storm to separate you from your party and bring you here."*

"You made the storm?" Zephyr asked. *"And a final test? What final test?"*

"Yes, I made the storm," the unicorn told Zephyr. *"To bring you here. You Princess Zephyr, have proven that you are pure of heart by first finding me. You have proven that you are brave by following me even when you knew that you were going to face great peril. Now, finally, you must prove that you are wise enough to govern the sword. Only then shall I reveal the sword to be claimed by a chosen and a new bloodline for the next century."*

"What must I do?" Zephyr asked as she stepped back with caution.

She was baffled and afraid of what the silver unicorn might say next.

"You must solve a riddle," the unicorn told Zephyr. *"You will have three opportunities and five minutes to answer the riddle correctly. If you fail to answer the riddle after three attempts or within five minutes, I shall touch you with my horn, and you will die."*

"Die?!" Zephyr repeated with a gasp. *"Why would I have to die?!"*

"You know too much, already," the unicorn replied. *"If you fail the final test, I cannot let you leave here without the sword and carrying the knowledge of what I have just revealed to you."*

"That's a bit harsh," Zephyr said. *"I don't know if I want to do it."*

"It is too late to turn back now. You must answer the riddle or die."

"But..." Zephyr started to say.

"Tell me when you are ready," the unicorn said as it cut Zephyr off.

Taking a deep sigh, Zephyr lowered her head sadly as she was filled with doubt and confusion.

But, she had no choice, and answering the riddle was the only way to recover the Sword of Wonders. So, exhaling, Zephyr tried to gather her wits as she stared at the silver unicorn.

"Okay," she said. *"I'm ready."*

"Good," the unicorn said.

Then, it backed up from Zephyr slowly.

"Now, for the riddle," the unicorn said, and Zephyr closed her eyes as she waited. And, the unicorn spoke.

"What has no shape but is more solid than the earth? What flows like water but can never be consumed? What has the strength of the strongest unseen wind but never dies down? What burns like fire but is hotter than any flame?"

"Alright," Zephyr said as she opened her eyes, and she held her chin as she entered deep thought.

"Where is Liz when you need her?" she told herself. "But, what would she do? A clue to the answer has got to be here somewhere?"

Turning, Zephyr examined the wood and clearing about her as she pondered on the silver unicorn's riddle.

However, a minute soon passed, and the unicorn took a step towards her.

"Oh no!" Zephyr said to herself as she wiped the sweat from her brow. "Think Zephyr!"

"Ugh!" she said as she threw up her hands with frustration. "The only thing here is the Tree of Life! Wait! That's it!"

"Is it life?" Zephyr asked the unicorn.

"No!" the unicorn said in a cold tone, and it took a step closer to Zephyr.

"So!" Zephyr said as she took a deep breath. "It's got to be something else!"

Holding her head, Zephyr thought and thought, but two more minutes passed, and the silver unicorn moved even closer to her.

Yet, though Zephyr didn't think that she would discover the answer to the riddle, she refused to give up, and after another half minute passed, she peered at the silver unicorn with desperation.

"Can't you give me more time?" she asked.

"No!" the unicorn replied coldly. *"I cannot!"*

Zephyr gritted her teeth as she wiped more sweat from her forehead, but after a second, she smiled as an idea came to her.

That's it!" she told the unicorn. *"That's the answer to the riddle! It's time!"*

"I'm afraid not!" the unicorn said as it drew closer to Zephyr.

Now, Zephyr only had one minute left to solve the riddle as well as only one guess, and the silver unicorn's horn was about an inch from her forehead.

Then, feeling defeated, Zephyr sank to her knees and sobbed as she put her head in her hands.

"Do not give up!" the unicorn told her. *"You can figure it out! You still have thirty seconds!"*

But, Zephyr simply shook her head.

"I will repeat it," the silver unicorn said softly. *"What has no shape but is more solid than the earth? What flows like water but can never be consumed? What has the strength of the strongest unseen wind but never dies down? What burns like fire but is hotter than any flame?"*

"I can't," Zephyr told the unicorn. *"I've let everyone down. Crystotopia, and the people I love. I've let them all down."*

Only seconds away from her death, Zephyr thought of everyone she cared about, and she closed her eyes as images flooded her mind.

She thought of her mother, her father, Syphron, Scorn, Helga, Brandon, Trinda, Elizabeth, and finally, she thought of Cor.

Opening her eyes, Zephyr watched as the unicorn's glowing horn was a moment away from touching her. Filled with emotion, Zephyr told the silver unicorn what she thought were her last words as tears fell rapidly down her face.

"Go on!" she said. *"Kill me unicorn! I don't know the answer to your riddle! I've come all this way, and I may have failed, but I know what matters! Everything I do is for the people I love, and love should be the answer to every question! It's what drives me, and I see that now! If it weren't for that, I wouldn't even be here! So, go ahead and take my life! But, my*

love will always exist! I only hope that everything I have done for the people I care about...I only hope that they will know the sacrifices I have made!"

Just as Zephyr spoke, the silver unicorn stepped back.

"What...what are you doing?" Zephyr asked.

"That wasn't a direct answer," the unicorn said. *"But, I'm willing to accept it. It was well-spoken and much better than the answer I was hoping for."*

"I don't know what you are saying," Zephyr said.

"It is simple," the silver unicorn said. *"Love is more solid than the earth. Love flows like water but cannot be consumed. Love has the strength of the strongest unseen wind, but never dies down. And, love burns like fire but is hotter than any flame. You have done well, Princess, and you have passed all of the tests successfully. Now, I will make the Sword of Wonders appear, and you may claim it."*

"I did it," Zephyr whispered.

"I did it!" she screamed as she jumped into the air and twirled happily.

The silver unicorn's horn began to glow even more radiantly, and heavy winds engulfed the ground in front of the Tree of Life.

Then, the earth shook roughly, and the silver and ruby-encrusted Sword of Wonders emerged from it as it began to levitate between Zephyr and the Tree of Life.

"The Sword of Wonders," Zephyr whispered.

Moving forward, she approached the sword.

But, just as her hand was inches away from touching it, a black beam of light hit Zephyr in the back forcing her to fall.

Her body was so sore from the attack that she could barely move.

Yet, mustering all of her strength, she turned to see Thantos flying down into the wood and clearing as he flapped his wings, and landed by the Sword of Wonders.

"A little too slow, Princess," he said with a cruel laugh. "Finder's keepers!"

"What are you doing, Thantos?!" Zephyr asked.

However, the fairy guard did not respond, and instead, he grabbed the hilt of the Sword of Wonders.

Then, the sword emitted a bright light that blinded Zephyr, and she covered her eyes.

When Zephyr could again, she gasped as Thantos held the sword up triumphantly.

"At last!" he said with a grimace. "The Sword of Wonders and all its might are mine!"

"Thantos!" Zephyr yelled as she struggled to stand. "What's wrong with you?!"

"Nothing is wrong, Princess," Thantos said as he grinned at Zephyr. "And, the name isn't Thantos, by the way. It's Scorpius!"

A black light flashed, and Zephyr screamed as Thantos' appearance changed before her eyes.

With a ferocious and rough face, dirty dark chocolate skin, fierce black eyes, grisly gray hair, and yellow rotted teeth, Zephyr knew that Thantos was actually the wicked Scorpius, King of Ember and leader of the Dark Forces. And, with the Sword of Wonders in his hand, Zephyr knew that she was powerless to stop him.

Chapter 15

Darkness Falls

"Scorpius!" Zephyr said as she stepped back cautiously.

"Yes, my dear Princess!" Scorpius said as he felt the blade of the Sword of Wonders. "In the flesh!"

"Move aside!" the silver unicorn told Zephyr as it stood in front of her. *"I must stop him!"*

"Be careful!" Zephyr said.

"I can speak to animals too!" Scorpius told the silver unicorn.

"Guardian of the sword," he said as his black eyes flashed.

"That sword was not meant to be claimed by you!" the unicorn said. *"This is a secret location, and I cannot allow to you live for coming here!"*

"Correction, unicorn!" Scorpius said with a hiss. *"After I intercepted the party that Lionus sent to Aeria, I reasoned that Princess Zephyr was the one who would lead me to the Sword of Wonders, and I waited near the Great Stair, knowing that she would come in search of the Oracles' advice. But, unfortunately for poor Thantos, he wandered a little too far away from his friends when he was scouting the land to see if it was safe, and consequently, I killed*

him and took his identity. *It is true that the Princess was the one whom you unicorn chose to test to see if she was worthy to receive the Sword of Wonders. Without her, I wouldn't have been able to find you or follow you to Brith. And, once you used your magic to reveal the location of the Tree of Life, it became accessible to anyone who was lucky enough to find it. And, though I was a little worried, the Princess solved your riddle and passed your final test. And, that was when you made the Sword of Wonders available to be claimed. But, there is no rule or law that says that 'I' can't enter the location of the Tree of Life once it has been revealed or claim the Sword of Wonders after it has been unearthed. This just isn't the Princess' lucky day, I'm afraid."*

"Perhaps there isn't a rule to stop you from claiming the Sword of Wonders," the silver unicorn said. *"However, you are forgetting that as the guardian of the sword, it is my duty to protect it from people like you."*

"Then try and stop me!" Scorpius said with a cackle.

As the silver unicorn approached Scorpius slowly, its horn began to glow gold, lightning flashed in the sky, and a fierce wind started to blow.

"No, you don't unicorn!" Scorpius said sinisterly. *"You can't defeat me! Not now that I have the sword!"*

Scorpius pointed the Sword of Wonders at the silver unicorn, and the sword began to glow a deep black as strong winds started to push the unicorn back.

Then, a black light flew from the sword and surged through the silver unicorn's body, knocking it to the ground.

However, the unicorn's glowing horn grew even brighter, and it stood once more as it moved towards Scorpius.

"I said no!" Scorpius yelled, and more black light emerged from the Sword of Wonders and engulfed the silver unicorn. And, the unicorn lay down on the ground as it was both weakened and defeated.

Gliding over to the silver unicorn, Scorpius held the Sword of Wonders above it.

"You nor anyone else can stop me now," he said.

Then, he peered at Zephyr and smiled maliciously.

"A lesson to you, Princess," he told her. "This is what will happen to you if you get in my way!"

With all of his strength, Scorpius raised the Sword of Wonders high in the air and brought it down swiftly.

"No!" Zephyr screamed.

But, it was no use. The silver unicorn's horn was severed, and the unicorn fell limp and still.

Running forward, Zephyr sobbed as she bent over by the creature's side.

"Princess," the unicorn said in a faint whisper. *"Do not feel concern or grief for me. As I told you before, I will be here until the Tree of Life dies and this world is no more. But, I fear now that this Scorpius wields the Sword of Wonders and the power of the creator that the end is near. Our only hope is to stop him."*

Then, the silver unicorn fell silent, and though Zephyr was worried, she could still feel its pulse, though it was weak.

However, snowflakes began to descend from the sky, and they fell until they covered the silver unicorn's body completely. And, Zephyr noticed that several rubies fell from the Tree of Life as well, and she knew that the silver unicorn and the Tree of Life were dying.

"You monster!" she said as he glared at Scorpius. "There's only one silver unicorn in the world! To harm something so magical...you can't get away with this! Now, even the Tree of Life is starting to wither!"

"Ha!" Scorpius said. "You're so emotional, like your mother."

"I'll stop you!" Zephyr said as she took out Wind Chaser. "One way or another!"

"So," Scorpius said. "The art of Chimmera. You wish to fight me. We've already been down this path, Princess. But...if you insist."

Suddenly, in Scorpius' free hand, a long gold and silver whip appeared with glowing red marks on it.

"Fire Starter!" Zephyr said with a gasp.

She recalled Scorpius' weapon that he had used to defeat her right before he kidnapped Cor.

"You remember?!" Scorpius said. "Let me give you a proper greeting!"

Then, with a swift stroke, Scorpius brought Fire Starter down, and a pillar of flame sped towards Zephyr.

But holding up Wind Chaser, Zephyr focused on it and the pillar of flame, and as she released her weapon, winds pushed the flames away from her, and Wind Chaser shot towards Scorpius.

Yet, with a twist of his hand, Wind Chaser clashed against Scorpius' whip, and as he knocked the weapon backward, Zephyr caught it.

"So," Scorpius said. "You've gotten better. But let's just see how much."

With a few swings of Fire Starter, Scorpius sent several balls of flames at Zephyr. She scrambled to avoid them, and she was terribly upset by the destructive fires Scorpius was creating around the silver unicorn and the Tree of Life.

"You're beginning to annoy me," Scorpius said.

"I...I hope so," Zephyr said as she tried to catch her breath.

"Let's make this entertaining," Scorpius said. "Dance, Princess! Dance!"

Bringing his whip down at Zephyr's feet, Scorpius caused her to jump in various directions as flames sprouted from the areas of the ground that Fire Starter touched.

"That's more amusing," Scorpius said after a minute. "You're so light on your feet, Princess."

"Really?" Zephyr said angrily. "Let me show you my newest move. I call it the Finale!"

And then, pouring all of her concentration into Wind Chaser, Zephyr released it, though Scorpius was quick to attempt to counter her move with Fire Starter.

However, Scorpius was shocked as Wind Chaser created winds so strong that he was pushed back as the weapon clashed against his own, and he struggled to parry Zephyr's attack.

But pushing her hand forward, Zephyr caused Wind Chaser to break through Fire Starter, cutting the whip in half, and Scorpius barely jumped aside to save his life.

Reaching down, he picked up half of the broken whip with a growl.

Then, as she focused, Zephyr used Wind Chaser to produce winds that put out the fires that Scorpius had created.

"Hmm," she said as she caught her weapon. "I guess I was good enough to beat you huh?"

"Enough with the games, Princess," Scorpius said as he tossed the remains of his weapon aside.

Then, he raised the Sword of Wonders, and a black light flashed that swept Zephyr off of her feet.

"You should be more worried about yourself," he told her. "And, I'm positive you're interested in the battle currently raging on in Crystotopia. How about I give you and your little friends a close-up?! I want you to witness its fascinating conclusion!" Scorpius turned the Sword of Wonders sideways, and the rest of her party and friends appeared.

"Zephyr!" Brandon said as he peered around curiously. "What's happening?!"

161

"It's Scorpius!" Zephyr said quickly. "He has the Sword of Wonders, and he was posing as Thantos!"

"I knew there was something funny about that fairy guard!" Trion said.

"That man is scaring me!" Tarn said nervously.

"No!" Sir Gallan said as he shook his head. "It can't be!"

Standing, he tried to charge at Scorpius, but he was still injured from the tree branch that fell on him, and he tumbled over in pain.

"Just wait and see what I'm going to do next!" Scorpius said.

He raised the Sword of Wonders into the air, causing a large black vortex to form in the ground.

Before Zephyr and her friends could act, they were pulled into the vortex with Scorpius.

Then, Zephyr and her friends were expelled from the vortex in the middle of the battle in Crystotopia in various directions.

And, because of the fighting taking place, Zephyr and her friends scattered as they tried to find shelter in all the chaos.

"Zephyr look out!" Brandon yelled, and he pulled both her and himself out of harm's way just as flames engulfed where she had been standing.

Brandon tried to use his crystal sword to put out the blaze, but it was no ordinary fire, and as Zephyr looked up, she found Cor hovering in the sky with flames all around him. Then, she knew that the fire was really caused by the power of the Great Flame of Ember.

"It's Cor!" Liz said loudly as she crawled over to Zephyr and Brandon. "He's using the Great Flame of Ember I take it."

"Your Highness," Helga said with a fearful voice as she dived on to the ground next to Zephyr. "I'm so scared!"

"I'm sure I can figure something out," Zephyr said. "I hope so anyway."

Peering up, Zephyr saw Trinda running towards her, but Trinda stopped suddenly as her eyes widened with fear.

"Oh no!" she yelled, and Zephyr, Helga, Liz, and Brandon looked behind themselves to see a man in green armor running towards them with a thick sword.

With dirty tan skin, menacing black eyes, and long dark black hair, Zephyr immediately knew him to be the Emerald Knight, Sir Waian.

"Not so fast Emerald Knight!" Sir Gallan screamed, and he stood in front of Sir Waian with his own sword, though Zephyr could see that he was still injured. But somehow, Sir Gallan had found the strength and will to fight.

"Oh, this is too good to be true!" Sir Waian said. "I'll skin you first, and then I'll take care of the kiddies!"

"I'm not afraid of you, Sir Waian," Sir Gallan said. "And, I will die protecting the Princess and her companions."

"I hope so," Sir Waian said.

Then, he and Sir Gallan clashed swords and started fighting each other to the teeth, and although Sir Gallan was injured, Sir Waian was already weary from battle, which somewhat evened the playing field.

However, it was still a brutal fight as Sir Gallan blocked many of Sir Waian's sword thrusts.

Sir Waian flipped into the air and landed behind Sir Gallan, but Sir Gallan was quick to swing his sword behind his back to block Sir Waian's next attack.

But, with another flip, Sir Waian kicked Sir Gallan in the head and stunned him as he moved backward.

Yet, as the Emerald Knight charged, Sir Gallan managed to do a roundhouse kick, and Sir Waian hopped into the air to avoid it as he landed nearby.

"So," Sir Waian said as he whirled his sword in the air. "I see that you still have a few tricks, Ruby Knight."

"Always," Sir Gallan said.

"Let's see you escape this!" Sir Waian yelled.

Running forward, he threw his sword, and as Sir Gallan ducked to block it, Sir Waian performed a jump kick that knocked Sir Gallan down.

Then, as the Emerald Knight pulled his sword from the ground, he turned to stab Sir Gallan. However, the Ruby Knight had managed to retrieve his own sword and clashed it against Sir Waian's weapon.

"Now," Sir Gallan said with a reddened face and clenched teeth. "Let's see you escape 'my' next move!"

And, with a magnificent parry, Sir Gallan forced Sir Waian's sword out of his hand. Before the Emerald Knight could recover his sword, Sir Gallan held his own sword at Sir Waian's throat.

"Don't kill me!" Sir Waian said. "You have won the battle fairly! I salute you, Ruby Knight!"

"Leave this place and never return!" Sir Gallan told Sir Waian.

"I can't..." Sir Waian started to say, but Sir Gallan moved his sword closer to his throat.

"I...I will go," the Emerald Knight said with a gulp.

Then, Sir Gallan sheathed his sword as he approached Zephyr and her friends.

"Are you alright?" he asked.

However, Trinda's eyes suddenly widened once more with terror.

"Behind you!" she screamed.

Sir Gallan turned just as Sir Waian's sword was about to go through his stomach, but before that happened, Sir Waian gasped and dropped his sword as he fell forward with a thud.

And then, everyone saw that behind Sir Waian, Brandon was standing petrified with his now bloodied crystal sword in his hand.

"Thank you, lad," Sir Gallan told Brandon as he put his hand on his shoulder.

"You're welcome," Brandon said as tears surfaced in his eyes. "I...I killed him. I've never killed another person before."

"You did what you had to do," Sir Gallan said as he cleaned Brandon's sword and gave it back to him. "There's no shame in it, and for once, I truly needed your help. Sir Waian only showed dishonor and a lack of virtue. But you, lad, before I said that maybe you might become a knight. Now I am going to say, that you most certainly will."

Sir Gallan smiled at Brandon, though Brandon remained stunned.

But then, the Ruby Knight's focus shifted as he examined the battlefield around him.

"You've got to get you and your friends out of here!" he told Zephyr. "You'll die if you stay!"

And, just as Sir Gallan said this, dark storm clouds formed in the sky, and Zephyr looked up to see Scorpius holding the Sword of Wonders.

"Get out of here now!" Sir Gallan screamed.

"Right!" Zephyr said.

"Brandon, Liz, Trinda, and Helga, hold onto me!" she told her friends. "I'm going to try the most powerful form of the transportation spell."

"But you tried that before at Letros' lair!" Trinda said. "And it didn't work!"

165

"Just do as I say!" Zephyr screamed as an explosion sounded a foot away from her.

So, Zephyr's friends obeyed her as they used their free hands to hold onto each other, and though Zephyr wasn't completely positive her spell would work, she was determined to try.

Closing her eyes, she was about to cast the spell, when flames shot over her head so hot that she nearly collapsed from their immense heat. Opening her eyes, Zephyr saw Cor attacking a group of fairy guards.

"Cor," she said in a whisper.

"Wait you guys!" she yelled. "I have to help him!"

Then, Zephyr's dangerously brown eyes flashed as she turned to face Helga, Trinda, Brandon, and Elizabeth.

"I have an idea that might get him to safety as well," she said. "Whatever happens, don't let go of me!"

"But Zephyr..." Trinda tried to say.

However, it was too late.

Closing her eyes once more, Zephyr pictured the area where Cor was floating above the ground, and she said loudly, "Transportus Maximus Executo!"

And, as Zephyr waved her hand above her head, everything vanished, and after a minute, Zephyr and her friends were standing next to Cor.

"No!" Helga screamed as she felt the intense heat generated from Cor's body and the flames around him. "We'll burn to death, Your Highness!"

"Hold on!" Zephyr yelled.

Reaching into the air, she grabbed Cor's hand, though her own hand started to burn and sear with pain.

166

And, as she closed her eyes, she did all she could to focus on and imagine the Forest of Difference. She pictured its colorful assortment of trees with various geometrically shaped leaves as well as its patches and areas of colored grass and bushes. Then, she said loudly, "Transportus Maximus Executo!"

Upon raising her own hand and rotating it while she gripped Cor's, Zephyr felt everything around her starting to disappear.

Just as she opened her eyes, the last thing Zephyr saw was a wave of black light sweep across the land knocking the allied kingdoms' armies off their feet.

But, a second before the wave of light hit her and her friends, everything grew dark, and the pain she felt from Cor diminished.

Soon, Zephyr and her friends were in the Forest of Difference, and amazingly, they were still alive.

"You did it!" Brandon said. "That was a little weird, but it worked!"

"Yes," Zephyr said as she felt her burned hand. "It did work, didn't it?"

"Let's not worry about that now!" Helga said nervously as she pointed behind Zephyr.

Everyone turned to see Cor floating in the air, and he didn't look happy.

"You are fools to stand in my way!" he said. "Now, you must die!"

"Cor no!" Zephyr screamed.

However, Cor aimed his hand at Zephyr, and flames formed a circle around her.

"Cor stop it!" Zephyr said. "You're under a spell! You're not really like this!"

"Less talking, more firing!" Cor yelled.

He pointed his hand at Zephyr again, and more flames flew towards her.

Waving her hand quickly, Zephyr thought, "Shieldus Maximus Executo!"

And, a giant gray shield of light formed in front of her just in time to block Cor's attack. However, the shield was no match for the Great of Flame of Ember, and Zephyr was knocked backward by the fire, and the flames were inches away from burning her.

"Cor please," Zephyr said as she stood and coughed from the smoke the flames caused. Also, she felt that the heat from the flames was unbearable.

"I love you," Zephyr said as she sobbed. "I care about you."

Flying forward, Cor hovered above her.

Zephyr raised her hand to cast another spell, but Cor grabbed her wrist and lifted her into the air.

"Zephyr!" Brandon yelled.

Trinda shot an arrow at Cor to stop him, but Cor burned it into dust before it reached him.

"Ahh!" Zephyr screamed as she felt heat flowing into her wrist and hand.

"I wonder how long it will take to cook you?" Cor said. "Let's find out!"

Reaching down, Cor wrapped his hand around Zephyr's other wrist. But as soon as he touched the golden friendship bracelet that Zephyr was wearing, he paused as memories seeped into his mind and consciousness.

"What...what is this?" Cor asked as he felt the bracelet. "I...I remember. I gave this to you for...for your birthday."

"Cor..." Zephyr started to say.

However, the pain she felt along with the heat of the flames and the smoke around her caused her to collapse.

"Zephyr!" Cor screamed.

Suddenly, Cor's hair stopped burning, and his eyes returned to their normal cinnamon color.

Landing, he put Zephyr on the ground gently. And, as he held up his hand, the flames surrounding him and Zephyr flew into the air and disappeared as they touched it. Next, Cor gripped the area of Zephyr's hands and wrists where he had burned her, and closing his eyes and concentrating, Zephyr's wounds were healed.

"What have I done?" Cor said as he felt Zephyr's hair. "I've done something terrible. I can tell."

"It wasn't your fault," Liz said. "Scorpius was controlling you."

"We have to revive Zephyr," Cor said. "Brandon, your sword."

"Okay," Brandon said.

With a swing of his sword, water poured over Zephyr's face, and she opened her eyes slowly.

"Cor," she said with a weak smile. "You're...you're okay."

"Yes," Cor said. "Thanks to you. But, I don't know what broke the curse. All I did was touch the friendship bracelet I gave you, and I remembered who I was. And somehow, I think I was able to use the Great Flame of Ember to heal your wounds. At least, the ones I caused."

"I'm glad I helped save you," Zephyr said as she started to cry. "But, I can't say the same for Crystotopia. I've failed. Scorpius has the Sword of Wonders, and he's already using it to destroy the allied kingdoms' armies. I don't know what we are going to do."

"It's okay," Cor said as he wiped the tears from Zephyr's eyes. "Whatever we do, we'll do it together. I'm here now."

Before Zephyr could say another word, she found herself kissing Cor on the lips.

"Oh," Helga said with a whimper. "I never thought I would see the day."

"Really, Helga," Zephyr said with a laugh.

"At least there's some good to come out of all of this, " she said as she rubbed Cor's face.

"Zephyr," Brandon said. "Can you contact Scorn?"

"I can try," Zephyr said. "But, I'm afraid to."

"We need some idea about what's going on," Liz said.

"Yes," Zephyr said hopefully as she rubbed her crystal ring. "We do, but it can't be good."

"Give it a chance," Cor whispered.

Zephyr closed her eyes and thought, "Sightus Impetus Exceuto!" and raised her hand. But, after a minute, nothing happened.

"It...it didn't work," Zephyr said nervously. "Scorn must be in trouble."

"You don't think he's...." Trinda started to say in a sad voice.

"He might be," Zephyr said softly.

"Maybe you didn't cast the spell right," Brandon said. "Try again."

Sighing, Zephyr closed her eyes and tried to cast the spell once more. But, it still didn't work.

"Oh!" Zephyr said as she shook her head. "Not Scorn."

Holding Zephyr, Cor patted her on the back.

"What now?" Liz said. "I don't think any logic can help us anymore. Magic can't either."

"I don't know, Liz," Zephyr said. "I don't know."

As Zephyr gazed into the sky, she saw that not even an ounce of sunshine was visible. However, it was only one of the signs of the darkness that had fallen upon Crystotopia as well as Danus. Zephyr and her friends no longer knew of any good that could come from their situation. The only thing they were truly sure of was that all they had...was each other."

The End

www.ingramcontent.com/pod-product-compliance
Lightning Source LLC
Chambersburg PA
CBHW061235170626
46809CB00007B/2693